# APRIL

## IN

# PARIS

# APRIL
# IN
# PARIS

*A NOVEL*

## JOHN J. HEALEY

Arcade Publishing · New York

Arcade Publishing books may be purchased in bulk at special discounts for sales promotion, corporate gifts, fund-raising, or educational purposes. Special editions can also be created to specifications. For details, contact the Special Sales Department, Arcade Publishing, 307 West 36th Street, 11th Floor, New York, NY 10018 or arcade@skyhorsepublishing.com.

Arcade Publishing® is a registered trademark of Skyhorse Publishing, Inc.®, a Delaware corporation.

Visit our website at www.arcadepub.com.

10 9 8 7 6 5 4 3 2 1

Library of Congress Cataloging-in-Publication Data is available on file.

Jacket design by Brian Peterson
Jacket photo credit: Getty Images

Print ISBN: 978-1-951627-74-4
Ebook ISBN: 978-1-951627-75-1

Printed in the United States of America

This is a work of fiction. Any resemblance to persons living or dead is purely coincidental.

For Soledad

# – Part One –

*A violent act is an epicenter; it shakes everyone within reach and creates other stories, cracks open the earth and reveals buried secrets.*

—Sarah Perry

– 1 –

A young girl in a dress. She's ten or eleven. I'm observing her, and at the same time, I *am* her. She holds a pair of scissors. An older, balding man with round glasses and a bow tie stands at her side. Both of them are looking down at a wire, a thick, taut, mercury silver wire. It's wrapped around the girl's ankles. She leans over and cuts it with the scissors. Although the older man does nothing to prevent it, the implication is that by cutting the wire she has done something wrong.

She runs out of a house. It's my maternal grandfather's home on Woodycrest Avenue in the Highbridge section of the Bronx, a brown, cedar-shingled, three-story house with yellow window frames. Terrified, she/I runs down the gray wooden front stairs and heads north. She/I is still holding the scissors, but now they're in two pieces, like kitchen shears that come apart, like two knives.

The terror comes from the fear someone is going to emerge from the house and pursue me. I'm trying to get to the corner and disappear before anyone can see where I'm going. I run along the sidewalk passing other, smaller houses. Each one has four cement steps and a narrow yard. Just as I reach West 165th Street and am about to go down toward Anderson Avenue, I wake up.

# - 2 -

The panic persisted for a few seconds until relief took its place. I was in my apartment on the Ile Saint-Louis—far, thank god, from the Bronx. Spring rain pitter-pattered on the panes of the tall, partly opened windows. The bedroom looked down at a cobblestone courtyard and a small fountain. I could hear the rain falling into it. Soothing sounds. It was the eighteenth of April, the day my mother died half a century ago, and the day my wife died, five springs past.

Why was I a young girl in the dream? Who was the balding man in the bow tie? Why did I escape by taking the long way? If I'd gone south on Woodycrest Avenue instead, there would only have been a single house between my grandfather's and the corner of West 164th Street. What were the wire and the scissor-knives all about?

I got up. I showered and dressed. I went out with an umbrella and got a baguette at La Boulangerie on the Rue Saint-Louis en L'île, and bought the papers at the Tabac and then some freshly squeezed orange juice at Les Vergers on the Rue des Deux Ponts. These and a handful of other establishments, French to the core, continued to provide the island with authenticity, bulwarks against a tide of otherwise commercial ventures aimed at tourists. I came back to the apartment along the Quai de Bethune and made breakfast. When the sun emerged, I opened all the banquette to ceiling window-doors in the living room facing the river, pulled up one of the heavy armchairs to take in the view, and sat down with my laptop.

A barge went by, then the day's first tour boat. I couldn't work. The dream wouldn't let me. Why that house? Embodying the young girl, what had I done wrong? It seemed all I'd done by cutting the wire was to free her, free myself.

The grandfather who owned the house was known to many as "the Judge." He had earned a small fortune in liquor distribution, and due to a large red nose, an ironclad liver, and dainty taste buds, he developed a knack for classifying whiskies. The skill had earned him the nickname. But given the context of the dream, the word "judge" probably reverted to its more legalistic meaning.

Years of analysis during my third decade had convinced me to accept the premise that, being prey to magical thinking and raised within a family averse to explanation, I blamed myself for my mother's death. She died of cancer when I was six years old. She had grown up in that house, had celebrated her marriage to my father there. After she died, I spent many nights sleeping in the room that had once been hers. So all of that was in play.

But there was something else. I could feel it.

# – 3 –

The Judge married young and had four children: a son who came nine months after the wedding, whom everyone called Paddy; then, years later, my mother, Aunt Moira, and my Aunt Jane. Paddy moved away and never married, Moira and my mother did marry, and Jane stayed home, single and stylish, taking care of her father. After my mother died, she took care of me for a time as well. I sent her a letter once expressing curiosity about what their mother had been like, a woman who had died long before I was born. Her reply, posted from a retirement home in East Hampton, was unexpectedly frank. I carried it around for years afterward, unaware that it contained clues. This is what it said.

*Dear Shaun,*

    *My mother, your grandmother, Elizabeth Monaghan, was born in 1886. Her father was born in Galway. Her mother was a good little Protestant girl from Onsala, Sweden. The Monaghans were gentle folk, very soft spoken and quiet. Grandpa worked in insurance and spent his final years in Riverdale. He was deaf by then but could read lips beautifully.*

    *Mom was much like your mother. Good humor, easygoing, preferred peace to bickering. But soon after I was born, she went through a rocky time with the Judge, became depressed, and developed a drinking problem. In 1916 she died of pneumonia in a rehab hospital. Your mother was ten and I was eight years old.*

*Your father and your mom grew up around the corner from each other. He and Paddy played together and your father's father, Grandpa Kerry, umpired their baseball games. Your parents didn't start dating until your mother was attending Teacher's College at Columbia University and your dad was in law school. They were married at Sacred Heart and the reception was at the house on Woodycrest Avenue. The Judge had a tent erected in the back yard, with a walkway constructed to connect to the dining room. The furniture was removed and there were flowers everywhere. It was lovely.*

*Your parents tried to have a child for twelve years. By the time you came along your mother had suffered many miscarriages. She took ill after you were born, and you were cared for by a nurse the first few months of your life. She was diagnosed with an ulcerated colon and treated with Sulphur, which was a new medicine. She was also advised not to have more babies.*

*Before you were born your parents lived at Nana's house at 1075 Ogden Avenue. I used to stop by every afternoon. I was at Mount St. Mary's then. After you were born, they moved to Undercliff Avenue. The summers in Southampton were special at Fair Lea and by then we had joined the Beach Club. Years later your mother complained of feeling lousy off and on. The doctor thought she was probably pregnant again but having experienced six pregnancies she didn't agree. The rabbit test was negative, and the doctor decided on an exploratory. Ovarian cancer was the immediate problem and the possibility of a damaged liver. That was in October.*

*In December she was admitted to St. Vincent's in Manhattan. When they operated, they saw the main artery to*

5

*the heart was involved. About all that could be done in those days was to insert a drain to the liver. It was before the transplants were invented. A cousin of your dad's stayed with you for the last couple of weeks while your mother was at home. She returned to the hospital about the 10th of April and died on the 18th. You stayed with Aunt Moira in Parkchester during the last week of your mother's illness and returned home after the funeral.*

*Love,*
*Aunt Jane*

- 4 -

For a long time, I played down my upbringing in the Bronx. It was a topic I avoided. I clung to the fact that my actual birth took place in Manhattan and that my mother and I went directly from the hospital to Southampton, Long Island. For my first thirteen summers the Judge and my father rented big houses near the beach. When Dad married again, Caro, his new wife, had her own house, an enormous "cottage" behind the dunes of Water Mill. I spent every June, July, and August I can remember at the Southampton Beach Club. But until my father remarried, I lived each fall, winter, and spring in the Bronx.

Irish and raised on Ogden Avenue, Dad became the borough's district attorney. His office was in the Bronx County Courthouse, which bordered the Grand Concourse across from Joyce Kilmer Park. I went to a Catholic school at the park's northern edge and was driven there each morning until the fifth grade by my father's chauffeur, a man named Gino Colossi who worked part-time cutting hair at his family barbershop that was also on Ogden Avenue.

After school I'd walk through the park to the courthouse and wait for Dad to finish his day. I'd do my homework at a desk next to his secretary, an elegant African American woman who lived in Harlem. She had beautiful hands and tried to teach me stenography, with little success. You could see the infield of Yankee Stadium out the window. Criminals in handcuffs paraded through the office regularly. The detectives adopted me as a mascot, fingerprinting me and showing me holding cells.

Dad was a friend of John F. Kennedy, Joe DiMaggio, and Gary Cooper. He also hung out with prizefighters, showgirls, and lawyers who defended gangsters. Sometimes before going to school I'd have breakfast with him at a coffee shop that had a soda fountain, tables and booths, and a brown stamped-tin ceiling. There was a wooden phone booth in the back. New York Yankees also breakfasted there before day games, which were the norm then and which my father always found time to attend, regardless of work. It was a place frequented by men: politicians, cops, detectives, lawyers, reporters, and ball players. I remember thick white plates of eggs, fried kidneys, hash browns, and bacon, mugs of coffee with spoons sticking out of them, guys with wide ties that stopped well short of their belt line, ruddy waiters behind the bar with long aprons. It was a place imbued with Irish testosterone, filled with weapons secured in scuffed leather holsters, briefcases with fading initials, thick-soled cordovan shoes, and university rings; men thickly built but light on their feet.

My school days were spent in fear of the Irish Christian Brothers, who taught me how to read and how to tell time. Whenever I made a mistake, they hit me on the hand with a leather strap or a ruler. When I did something that pleased them, they gave me holy cards. After school I played with toy soldiers, knights, and damsels in distress, watched TV, and was shuttled back and forth between the Judge's house and our apartment. And there were afternoons when I rode around the city in Gino Colossi's black Chrysler Imperial that smelled of White Owl cigars despite a sticky pine thing that hung from one of the radio knobs.

But the summers were different. Long before I was born, the Judge befriended Thomas Cuddihy. The Cuddihys were rich and one of the few Catholic members of the Southampton Beach Club. When I was three Mr. Cuddihy died and the Judge got close to his widow. She endorsed the Judge's entry to the Beach Club, and we became members as well. The Judge and my parents rarely went there. Along with Mrs. Cuddihy and the rest of the older Cuddihy generation, they preferred their own beach between Old Town Road and Phillips Pond. But I went to the Beach Club on my bike every day of every summer. I had lunch there. I swam in the ocean there. I swam in the pool. I played tennis with my summer friends on the grass courts at the Meadow Club up the road. Then when Dad married Caro, years after my mother's death, the Bronx was left behind. We moved from Undercliff Avenue in Highbridge into Caro's Fifth Avenue duplex facing Central Park. My father resigned his post and entered a law firm near Wall Street and worked there until he died.

But no matter what country or city I lived in afterward, the old neighborhood in the Bronx returned in my dreams. The dream that disturbed me in Paris that morning was not unusual in this regard. Given the date, perhaps the cutting of the wire was some sort of attempt to escape the guilt I felt about my mother's death, the fear I felt of being discovered and accused, the guilt and fear compounded by the relief I felt when my wife died after months of illness.

I'd recently finished reading Patrick Modiano's *Dora Bruder*. Perhaps the girl in the dream came from there. But Dora was an orphaned adolescent, and the girl I'd been in the dream was no older than eleven. I googled Woodycrest Avenue. What came up first was the gothic orphanage down the hill from the Judge's house, a creepy place I'd walked by countless times as a child. So that was one for Dora.

Then I remembered that as I was getting ready for bed the night before, I had heard a siren, a Paris siren, a sound I always associated with Nazis because I first heard it watching George Stevens's movie version of *The Diary of Anne Frank*. Was the young girl in the dress Anne Frank, waiting for the Nazis to grab her? The bald man with the round glasses and bow tie in the dream was a dead ringer for Ed Wynn, who interpreted the role of Mr. Düssel.

I thought about the scissors. Though they came apart like kitchen shears, they were actually more akin to the kind of scissors barbers use. In the context of my Bronx childhood, this led to a single source— Gino Colossi. He was practically considered family, a dapper little man with a pencil mustache who often told me I'd forget him one day, a prediction pretty much borne out until that morning.

On a lark, I googled "Colossi Barbershop." Only a few entries surfaced, but two caught my eye immediately. One actually included the name: Luigino Colossi. I clicked on it and found myself in the midst of a transcript of a murder trial in which Luigino Colossi had been a witness. But when I saw the trial date, 1916, I realized it must have been my Gino's father. There was also an eBay result, offering a 1934 photo of the barbershop. Seeing it there on my screen in the Paris apartment was unsettling. I recognized a very young version of the Gino I'd known, standing next to his namesake and brothers.

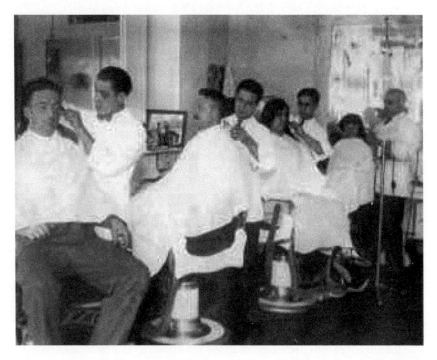

Then I googled the trial. Moments later I had a pdf of the whole thing. Instinct told me not to read it.

**4:10 p.m.** Trial Resumed

**Luigino N. Colossi** called as a witness on behalf of the People, being first duly sworn, testifies as follows:

"I am a barber, at 1066 Ogden Avenue, Highbridge. I have been in business there for thirty years. I remember the night of June 6, 1916, the night the body of Ingrid Anderson was found in the cellar of 1077. About 7:30 p.m. that night I was standing in front of my barbershop. I saw MacBride there. He came up to me and said, 'Gino, please lend me ten cents.' I said, 'Don't be shaming yourself asking me for ten cents. I have five children and a sick wife in the house. Why don't you have ten cents in your pocket?' I had been in the habit of lending him five and ten cents before that and he did not return it so well. I next saw him at the police station because I was called down there to testify to such things as I testify now."

I'd never met Gino's father. He died long before I was born. Nevertheless, I was riveted by the testimony. The trial went on.

"**I am Albert Boulder**, the janitor of the premises 1075 and 1077 Ogden Avenue. This is at Highbridge, in the borough of the Bronx, in the County of New York. I have been janitor there for fifteen years. They are double tenement houses, five stories each, with ten families in each house. Under these houses there are basements. In that basement there are storerooms. The janitor's apartment is also on that floor that connects both houses and there is an entrance to my apartment from both the houses.

"I know the family of Mrs. and Mr. Anderson. They lived in 1075. I also know a family named Conlan. They lived in 1077 on the third floor. I know the defendant. He lived with the Conlans. The Andersons lived on the third-floor rear of 1075.

"I remember the day and night of June 6, 1916. I had heard about the Anderson girl being missing. I went down to the cellar to fix the hot water heater around ten. Something attracted my attention. The door to the coal room was open about five inches. I saw part of a shoe. When I opened the door, I saw the child lying there partly covered with an old quilt that belonged to me and which I stored there. The covering came down to the breast. The lower part of her body and legs were uncovered. The head had been shoved between the stove and the wall, and that left the legs hanging together, but crossways to the door. I did not remove the covering at the time. I ran out and told my wife and Mrs. Buckley. She was on the 1075 stoop. She is one of the tenants and lives in 1075. Then I went over to the firehouse across the street to telephone the police."

## 6

I was interrupted at this point by a phone call from Shanghai. It was a German woman I had dated earlier that year. She was coming back to Paris and hoped to see me again. She was lovely to look at but devoted to international finance—I'd found her more taxing to talk to than I had originally hoped when I first approached her at a gallery opening. I made excuses, trying to be as friendly as I could, and then I went right back to the transcript.

> "**I am Dr. Daniel Black.** I reside at 1046 Ogden Avenue. I am a physician. I remember the night of June 6, 1916, when I was summoned to 1077 Ogden Avenue. It was about ten o'clock. I went down to the cellar from the street. There were a number of people present, but I can't remember who they were. I looked into the coal room and saw the body of a child lying on its right side, with its face toward the stove, in between the stove and the wall.
>
> "I removed the quilt and pulled the child's body out just far enough to listen to its heart. I placed it on its back. I discovered that the child was dead, that there was mucus and saliva and a little blood coming from the nose and mouth, and marks on the throat. There was a large bruise, I think on the left side, just above the larynx, and on the other side there were two or three marks which looked like fingerprints. On the right side of the

throat, I saw some marks that looked like the imprint of fingernails.

"I made a further examination of the body and the clothing. I had to lift up the skirt to do so. When I lifted up the skirt, I saw the privates. I only examined the condition of the under-clothes. Outside of that I made no examination, although at the time I lifted the skirt, I had that in mind. I did not make a fur-ther examination for rape because I did not think it the proper place to do it. The drawers were down far enough to expose the privates. And she had soiled herself—the bowels had moved. It is usual, by death ensuing and the relaxation of the system, that anything in the bowels is exuded. That is almost always the case. After I saw this, I turned the skirt down again, and put the quilt under the body, so that it would not rest on the cellar floor."

"**I am John August Anderson.** I reside at 214 West 148th Street. I was born in Sweden. I have been in this country twelve years. I am a metal worker and have been employed by the Consolidated Gas Company for about nine years. I am married. In June 1916, I was living with my wife and family at 1075 Ogden Avenue. At that time, I had two children. My oldest child's name was Ingrid Anderson. She was eleven years seven months old in June. The younger child's name is Adranaxa Anderson. He is nine years and seven months old. I lived at that address since March 15, 1916.

"I remember the evening of June 6. I arrived home at ten minutes to seven. My children usually met me as I came up the street. On this evening my children did not meet me. I found the little boy in the kitchen. My wife was home. The little girl was not there.

"After supper I went out to look for the girl. I went around the block, where there are some empty lots, and I looked there. Every place I saw children playing I asked if they had seen the child. At eight I went home again. She was not there. We then went down Ogden Avenue to Central Bridge that cuts across the Harlem River there. There is a park there. We did not find her. Then we went to the house again. We learned nothing there. All the people around were neighbors. None of them had seen her.

"Then I went to the police station. From the station house I went home again, a little after ten. There was a crowd there. I went down into the cellar. The officers and the doctors were down in the cellar. I saw my little girl, Ingrid. The dress was up, and the drawers were down, and she was dead. She had a white dress on and a red sweater."

"**I am John Cupperman, MD.** I am a coroner's physician in the borough of the Bronx. On Friday, June 7, 1916, I performed an autopsy on the body of the child identified to me as Ingrid Anderson, at her residence, 1075 Ogden Avenue, Highbridge.

"The apparent age of the child was ten or eleven years, rather small build, slightly developed, blonde. She was female. We removed the clothing and I examined the body for external evidences of death. The usual evidences of death were there, but in addition to that, there were some marks upon the back of the neck that consisted of bruises. The bruises were of the size and shape such as could have been made by an adult's hand.

"I opened the body from the chin down to the pubes, that is the point at the pelvic bone; made one incision right through the structures and laid the structures bare. The several structures of the throat I removed in mass, that is the tongue, posterior wall of the pharynx, and the larynx and the trachea, all of the structures of mastication and respiration in the pharynx, and then carefully dissected them apart to observe their relation and any change there was from the normal. The lungs were also removed at the same time, and the heart.

"I found upon examination that the hyoid bone, which is situated at the base of the tongue, had been broken. In my opinion the cause of the breaking of this bone was a traumatism of some kind. The lungs were removed and examined and found to be very much congested and edematous. That means in plain English that the little air vesicles in the lungs were filled up with a watery, serous fluid that exudes from the blood vessels.

"The heart was normal, kidneys normal, all of the organs of the body were normal. I have not the slightest doubt but what her death was caused by strangulation. It would take a period of at least two or three minutes, the very minimum, to cause the condition that I found here, namely this broken bone, these marks on the throat, the condition of the tongue, the blood, the mucus and the mouth and the edema of the lungs.

"I also found evidence of violence with reference to rape. I examined the body for that purpose. The genital organs were not intact and there was evidence of bleeding. I didn't make a microscopic examination at that time. I looked for that purpose in the genital organs and found disturbing evidence."

## 7

My father, I realized, was born the same year as Ingrid Anderson. A midwife delivered him to the world in the same house where Ingrid lived and died. 1075 Ogden Avenue is near the corner of West 165th Street, the one I ran to in my dream. I was headed for Anderson Avenue when I woke up. Was the girl in my dream Ingrid Anderson? It was difficult to believe.

My father surely knew her and might have played with her. My paternal grandparents, Nana and Pop Kerry, both of them born in Ireland, had stored some of their things in the basement where Ingrid was raped and strangled. They knew the neighbors, the Conlans where this MacBride fellow lived, Mrs. Buckley, and the janitor, Albert Boulder. It was more than likely that Doctor Black was their physician. Their apartment faced the backyard of 1075 and was two stories tall, which is to say, they lived directly under the Andersons.

I knew the house. I had visited it many times. I had slept there. Nana and Pop lived there until they died in the early 1970s. It was near my mother's house on Woodycrest. How did this grisly murder affect my father and his parents and brothers? The United States had just entered World War I. My mother was young, but surely the case was well known to everyone in the neighborhood. It happened the same year the Judge's wife died. How had it affected Luigino Colossi Jr.— Gino—who'd driven me to school for so many years? I would have sworn I'd never been told about it. But the dream indicated that I had.

I remembered my father's parents reading gruesome stories from the newspapers out loud to each other in their thick Irish accents, grisly tales from the *Daily News* and the *Daily Mirror*. Maybe they told me about Ingrid. There were many opportunities. I'd sit with them at the kitchen table that was covered with oilcloth, shiny white with little green shamrocks on it, stained with tea mug rings. When I was Ingrid's age Pop Kerry took me on walks down by the New York Central train tracks that ran along the Bronx side of the Harlem River. Nana would sometimes sequester me in her bedroom to tell me stories about her childhood in County Clare and share her favorite snack of raisins with butter.

It was shocking to read how the Bronx coroner's physician performed the autopsy in the children's bedroom while the girl's parents and little brother sat in the adjacent parlor. It was almost as invasive, indecent, and perverse as the crime that killed her. Removing her clothes, opening her up with his scalpel "from the chin to the pubes," pulling out her tongue, larynx, and pharynx with a single grasp, then her trachea and lungs, cutting out her heart and kidneys. Where were these severed, glistening organs—or "structures" as he called them—placed? On the bed? A table? On the scuffed wooden floor? There was no bathroom nearby, no scrubbed tiles or rubber gloves, no sterilized aluminum trays. It was June in a building with scant ventilation. I found it appalling.

The testimony referring to the manner of death was equally macabre. Strangulation is always abbreviated in the movies. One becomes accustomed to theatrical shorthand. Reading the declarative sentences of the transcript describing how it would have taken two to three minutes to murder the girl—an eternity for victim and assassin—pressing upon her little throat so intensely that the hyoid bone broke, that the killer's fingernails left bloody wounds, was revolting. I wondered if he'd done it looking at her face or from behind.

And the father, John August Anderson, had worked for the Consolidated Gas Company. That name sounded familiar. I ran a search and discovered it was basically owned by Thomas E. Cuddihy, my stepmother Caro's multimillionaire father, the man whose widow got the Judge and my parents into the Beach Club, the head of the Cuddihy-Woodward clan in Southampton that owned almost all the land south of Wickapogue Road. Might there be a connection between the Cuddihys and this grisly murder? The possibility freaked me out.

I scrambled eggs for lunch and remembered something else—and thought it curious I'd forgotten—a book given to me by a friend on my arrival in Paris in January, when my sabbatical started. *L'Age d'homme*, by Michel Leiris. My friend gave it to me because its final chapter is a rumination inspired by *The Raft of the Medusa*, the painting by Theodore Géricault that I was writing about. I'd been commissioned to contribute a chapter in a catalog for the Louvre to accompany an exhibition planned for the 200th anniversary of when the painting was first shown there.

I retrieved the book from my bedside table and found the part pertinent to the dream:

> One of the earliest memories I have is of the following scene:
> I am ten or eleven years old and at school; on the same bench
> with me is a girl in a gray velvet dress, with long curly blonde
> hair; we are studying a lesson together in the same *Sacred History*
> text. I still see quite clearly the illustration we were looking at; it
> represented Abraham's sacrifice; above a kneeling child with
> clasped hands and exposed throat hovers the patriarch's arm,
> wielding an enormous knife, and the old man raises his eyes to
> heaven, seeking the approval of the wicked God to whom he is
> sacrificing his son.

I made an effort to put the entire morbid business of the trial behind me and worked for a couple of hours. Later I rewarded myself with an afternoon walk. If you leave my place and cross the Seine onto the right bank and head northeast toward the Bastille or the Gare de Nord, it's unsightly. If you cross to the left bank and head east toward the Gare de Austerlitz, you fight your way against racing cars and taxis or hug a drab slice of river. What I mostly did, and had been doing the past few days, was to cross the Pont Marie and head into the Marais.

Though its narrow sidewalks, jammed with pedestrians stream-ing past expensive boutiques, hip bars, and specialty shops were unfriendly to foot traffic, the generally chic and attractive appear-ance of almost everyone and everything made up for it. Orthodox Jews also lived in the neighborhood, and there was the Shoah Memorial, the exquisite dimensions of the Place des Vosges, and the noble architecture of the National Archives with its graveled paths and sculpted *Last Year at Marienbad* fir trees. I mostly went to the Marais to buy wine at the Caves du Marais, then salmon and pasta at the Autour Saumon, or to grab a light lunch at Le Café Suédois across from the little park, the George Cain Square, where young mothers looking like fashion models were inevitably glued to their phones sitting next to thousand-euro baby carriages.

But on that afternoon, I opted for another route. I crossed over the Seine to the Left Bank and took the Rue de Pontoise to the Boulevard Saint-Germain. Then I went up the Boulevard Saint-Michel toward the Luxembourg Gardens. My impressions of the Boulevards Saint-Germain and Saint-Michel had evolved over time. At first, in my teens, they were iconic, literary avenues, romantically imagined before I ever crossed the Atlantic. I envisioned them, inspired by Flaubert's *Sentimental Education*, Henry Miller's *Tropic of Capricorn*, and Hemingway's *A Moveable Feast*, as wide streets that, along with the Tulleries and the Eiffel Tower, evoked a sepia-toned, eroticized Paris. The power of these reveries was such that, even as I first began to walk along them, I continued to see them as I wished. Although brief sections rose to the level of my fabrications—the block encompassing the immutable Café Flore, for instance, and the now tragically extinct La Hune bookstore, or the polychrome architecture of the Saint-Michel fountain and the no-nonsense staff at the Café Le Luxembourg—by my fourth or fifth visit I could no longer maintain any illusions regarding these streets. They were a disappointment. As had happened on the Ile, and to so much of Paris, with the exception of a few restaurants and classic stores managing to hang in there, most of the storefronts on these boulevards had been taken over by high-end franchises and eateries aimed at tourists. I was so used to it by then I hardly noticed. It was simply Paris.

The Luxembourg Gardens, on the other hand, preserved and conserved with old-school Gallic severity, continued to be a reliable and consoling destination.

I'd been drawn to its gardens, a bastion of civilization, since my late teens. The temperature and the light that day were ideal. Everything felt fresh and green from the morning rain. The bronze statue of Pan cheered me. The chestnut trees were in blossom. I sat in one of the chairs, the kind Henry James called "penny chairs," on the terrace overlooking the grand circular fountain where toy sailboats skimmed about.

I stretched my legs, relaxed, and looked forward to the evening. Unattached for more than a year and disillusioned from what had been an initial spurt of dating that winter, I'd gotten used to savoring my time alone. But a dinner party now and then was much appreciated, and one awaited me a few hours later. My hosts lived two doors down the Quay; perfect for someone like me who was lazy about traversing Paris at night. I didn't know them that well, they were more friends of friends, but we kept running into each other at the food shops and one thing had led to another. He was a well-known filmmaker from New York, Dirk Salisbury, a sort of uber preppie, married to an heiress from Spain. I wondered what "Dirk" came from, whether it was his real name or stolen from Dirk Bogarde, whom he slightly resembled. I also associated the name with an old-fashioned dagger, an image that suited him. His wife was named Consuelo and they had a young daughter, Lucia, who attended school on the Ile. It was to be an evening of relaxed conversation and good food.

Back at the apartment that evening, after I'd dressed for dinner, I poured myself a glass of wine and found myself being drawn back into the trial transcript.

***

"**I am Fred Hulberg.** I am an undertaker. I was called in to take care of the remains of Ingrid Anderson. I went to the premises at 1075 Ogden Avenue. She was in a side room, a bedroom. I folded the clothes she'd been found in right on the floor near the window and the wardrobe. I made no alterations to them or put anything on them. We dressed the child's body with a dress the mother provided and placed the child in the casket. The father and mother were present at the time. I went to the house again on Sunday, the day of the funeral. The funeral was to take place at a church. The body was taken out from the parlor."

"**I am Elsa Anderson.** I reside at 214 West 148th Street. I am the mother of Ingrid Anderson. I have been married to my husband for twelve years. At the time of her death Ingrid was eleven years and seven months and fifteen days. I bought or made and took care of her clothes. I was acquainted with the child's clothing.

"On the night of her death I did not go down into the cellar. I went as far as the stairs, but my husband would not let me in. The first time I saw my girl's body was on Saturday when she was in the casket. I did not see her when she was brought up that night, nor when she was put in the bedroom. The funeral took place on Sunday. On Monday I went back to the flat with my husband. I saw the clothes she'd been wearing when they found her folded in the corner of the room where the undertaker had put them. My husband and I put them in the laundry bag. They were in the bag until the next day, when they were given to the officer. Before I put the clothes in the bag, I looked at them, and I saw that the buttonholes of the petticoat and the drawers were torn.

"I know the defendant by sight. I have seen him pass by in the neighborhood. I saw him in the Bronx court. I saw him on the night I was searching for my child about eight o'clock. He was sitting on the curbstone, near the real estate office. I think he was alone. He did not say anything to me."

## 9

That was enough for one day. I left my building and took in the fading twilight on the river. It was at Dirk and Consuelo's that evening that I met Carmen. Perhaps the strength of my reaction to her had something to do with the aforementioned period of abstinence, that and the bracing fresh air she represented after a strange and unsettling day. She was slight and had a shock of blonde hair. If I'd been pressed, I would have pegged her as some sort of aristocrat from Northern Italy.

"This is a setup," she said to me not long after Dirk made the introductions.

"I see that."

"You'd no idea."

"None."

"They've not done this sort of thing to you before?"

"No," I said. "It's an area of my life I normally pursue on my own."

"So it will probably be a disaster," she said, making a face.

Like me, she was nervous and uncomfortable with the "setup," as she called it. Her voice was low and had a slight British lilt. She wore a chic black cocktail dress and a pair of silvery sandals.

"What can I get you to drink?" Dirk barked at me. He was in a navy blazer that had fleur-de-lis enameled buttons, a striped shirt, faded jeans, and red espadrilles. He had a handsome, narrow, well-defined face and short graying hair.

"Do you have *any* good wine?" I asked. "Dirk has this theory," I explained to Carmen, "trumped up to disguise chronic cheapness, that inexpensive wines are just as good as reserve cuvées, and that if you pay more than ten bucks for a bottle . . ."

"You're an idiot," he said, finishing my sentence. "Believe me," he said, shaking his head at us, "it's all marketing bullshit."

"What are you drinking?" I asked Carmen.

"Vodka on the rocks," she said, raising a tumbler for my inspection.

"Smart," I said. "I'll take the driest white wine you've got Dirk, with an aspirin chaser."

"Oh, she's smart all right," Dirk said, unscrewing the top from a scarily generic Sauvignon Blanc I recognized from the Moroccan mini-mart up the street. "She's much smarter than you or me. I predict a Nobel Prize in this *señorita*'s future."

"I think Dirk believes that if you teach anything in the sciences, you're automatically a genius," she said.

"Neither he nor I are especially fluent in that area," I said. "But what his comment is mostly alluding to is his opinion that art history—my field—is for slackers."

He grinned and handed me the bad wine poured into a beautiful glass. He was nursing a scotch. I suspected he'd gotten a head start in the drinking department.

"After seeing him around the neighborhood for a while I was formally presented to Dirk by a mutual friend who also has a place on the Ile," I said to Carmen.

"Another American?"

"Yes."

"Are there any French left on the island?" she asked.

"A few," I said.

"Most," Dirk chimed in. It was a topic he was touchy about.

"Anyway," I said, "this fellow, this mutual friend, comes from a family of famous publishers, newspapers and magazines mainly, including the inexplicably still surviving *Town & Country*. Do you know it?"

"Vaguely."

"The last time the three of us had a meal together—two years ago, Dirk?—Dirk says to him, 'I've canceled my subscription.' Our friend, who could not have cared less, asks, 'Why?' and Dirk says, 'Since the day I got an issue with a couple on the cover who were from Atlanta.'"

She laughed, the smallest bit, which relieved me. Dirk of course was pleased by the *homage* to his advanced snobbery. But I felt uncomfortable for having told the anecdote, too like one of the prosperous gauche Americans she'd referred to.

Consuelo appeared with Lucia, who was blonde and eleven years old, like Ingrid Anderson, but very much alive. Consuelo wore black suede heels, orange raw silk trousers, and a white blouse. Mother and daughter had their hair cut short. Kisses were exchanged.

"What do you think of my *amiga*?" Consuelo asked.

"Your *amiga* is a most pleasant *sorpresa*," I said.

"We've known each other since we were Lucia's age."

"I wish you'd warned me," I said. "I would have dressed better."

"We were afraid you might not come at all."

"Well, I'm glad I did," I said, still feeling somewhat like a fuddy-duddy.

"What would you have worn different?" Carmen asked.

"A burgundy velvet smoking jacket perhaps, and a pair of matching slippers."

"I've just the thing in my closet," Dirk piped up.

"I bet you do," I said.

As the evening went on, I learned that Carmen was from an old Catalan family, that she had gone to some progressive school in Madrid with Consuelo, who was also Catalan, when they were little. Years later they'd found themselves living in New York at the same time and resumed their friendship. They shared an overlapping social life in Manhattan, even though their professional worlds were very different. Consuelo worked for a film producer in Tribeca back then, which was how she met Dirk. Carmen was getting a PhD in microbiology at Columbia. Later she transferred to MIT, where she had tenure and a titled professorship.

After Lucia played us a rendition of "Clair de lune" on the piano, followed by a vigorous Scott Joplin rag, we sat down to dinner.

"I'm grateful for a home-cooked meal," Carmen said. "After staying with my mother in Madrid I've been in hotels the past few days."

"It's just pasta and a salad," Consuelo said.

"With shaved truffles," Dirk added.

"And red wine that actually comes in a bottle," I said, "though perhaps you've transferred it from a carton in the kitchen."

"You'll never know," he said, then added, "Shaun is due for a home-cooked meal too, I imagine."

"You don't cook?" Carmen said to me.

"I go out a lot," I said.

"And when he doesn't," added Dirk, eager to reach his anecdote, "he orders take-out from the Tour d'Argent. The waiters walk it over, serve him, and clean up afterward."

"Sounds very civilized," Carmen said.

"Thank you," I said, glad of a chance to look at her again.

"Vulgar would be more the word," Dirk said.

"You're just jealous," said Consuelo.

"I don't do it *that* often," I said. "It's just that I'm a terrible cook."

I continued to fear I was coming off wrong. I hoped that whatever Consuelo had reported in my favor beforehand might still be shoring me up. Then Lucia told us about some of her schoolmates. Dirk talked about a new film, a costume drama he would be shooting in Ireland that summer. Consuelo and Carmen reminisced about their early school years in Madrid, what had become of this and that person, who had married whom, and then went on to tell war stories from their days in New York. I was content to drink my wine and listen.

"Shaun has a huge apartment on Fifth Avenue," Dirk suddenly blurted out, "that he doesn't even use when he goes there."

"Why is that?" Carmen asked, genuinely intrigued.

"It came with my marriage," I said, unprepared for this topic. "I associate it more with my wife's former life and family. So it just sits there. I mean it's kept clean."

"How extraordinary," she said.

"I don't go to New York that often anyway," I said. "It doesn't feel like my city anymore. I prefer a hotel."

"Carmen's divorced," Dirk said, apropos of nothing. "And has no children and no boyfriend at the moment that we know of."

"I don't tell you everything," Carmen said, and she blushed.

"Oh-oh," Dirk replied.

"Shaun's wife died," Lucia said.

Everyone looked down.

"Lucia," her mother said in a tone of gentle admonishment.

"That's all right," I said. "It's been a while now."

"I'm sorry," Carmen said.

"Thank you," I said. "But surely they've told you all about that."

"Some," she said.

"What else have you told her?" I asked my hosts, with what I hoped was a convincing smile.

"Very little you'll be pleased to know," said Dirk. "Very little from me. I can't speak for Consuelo. I've only reported the basics. Your repulsive wealth, of course, and that you're overdue for a real relationship. Oh, and that you 'work' at the Clark Museum and teach the occasional boring art history class at Williams College, only a three-and-a-half-hour drive from MIT."

"Both of you are only children and neither of you have any presence on social media," Consuelo added. "I found that intriguing and told her that. But I also told her we really don't know you that well."

"You're at the Clark," Carmen said.

"Yes. Do you know it?"

"I've been up in the area and visited it once. The grounds are so beautiful."

"This after many years teaching at NYU's Institute of Fine Arts and a turn at the Met, he should add," said Dirk, pointing at me with his fork.

"Not that many years," I said.

"I hear Williams has a good science department," said Carmen.

"Yes, I've heard the same thing. I'm sure it's true," I said.

"You don't know?" She was surprised.

"I keep to myself. I mostly live in Lenox and commute. But tell me about your field. What is it you teach or do research on?"

"*Bof*," she said, dismissing my query in a Parisian manner. "I'd rather hear about Géricault. You're writing something on him, no?"

"Yes."

"Full disclosure," she said. "I read your profile on the Clark website."

"Ah," I said, pleased but worried. The staff photograph had been taken ten years earlier and I had a lot more gray in my hair the evening the picture was taken.

31

"There's no point in her trying to tell us what she does," Dirk said, "because we won't understand it. Not a word. I've already tried."

"I mostly study proteins," she said, "and how they fold."

"I read something about that," I said. "The folding determines their shape and the shape determines their function."

"That's right," she said.

Dirk's mouth fell open in an exaggerated fashion.

After we thanked them and said goodnight, we walked along the river. We passed the door to my place, but I was too embarrassed to point it out, seeing how close it was to Dirk and Consuelo's.

"Where are you staying?" I asked her.

"On the Rue Jacob," she said. "At the Angleterre."

"Let me walk you there."

"That's very gentlemanly of you."

We continued toward the prow of the Ile, past the ever-present crowd in a line for Bertillon ice cream, and crossed over the Pont Saint-Louis, skirting what remained of the gardens behind the burned-out ruins of Notre Dame.

"So far so good, no?" I said at one point.

"With regard to . . ."

"The setup," I said.

She just smiled. We passed a young couple making out. Rather than please or inspire me, or to take it as a good omen, it deepened my case of nerves.

"Ah, Paris," was all I could think to say. She did not respond.

We crossed the Pont de l'Archevêché, where all of the lovers' locks had been removed, and made our way up to Shakespeare & Co. Traversing the Rue Saint-Jacques, we ducked into the Rue de la Huchette, making our way past cheesy, raucous kabob restaurants filled with tourists, and headed for the Rue Saint-André des Arts. I mentally saluted what was left of the Grand Hotel Mont-Blanc. It was the first place I stayed on my own in Paris when I was nineteen. It had been converted from a bordello and all the rooms were decorated differently. Mine was basically pink with cherubs, a canopied bed and a mirror you stared up at, a bad carpet, and a fake Louis XV desk. A minuscule sink in the corner had been the only recourse for ablution. It wasn't especially clean, but that too was part of its charm. A large black-and-white photo of Pablo Neruda had hung behind the reception desk. The glow from the two weeks that I stayed there, my initiation into Left Bank Parisian life, had never really left me.

We took the Rue de Buci to the Rue de Seine and swung up to the Rue Jacob. She stopped to admire some clothing on display in the window of the Isabel Marant boutique and as she did, I stepped back to admire her. I was excited to be with her, talking about inconsequential things. Further on we both looked at framed letters for sale written by famous dead people in the windows of a store called something like Autographes et Documents Historiques. One of them was signed by Proust, another by Charles Dickens, a third by Josephine Bonaparte. In each case the handwriting was even and legible in a way that no one achieved anymore. We reached the entrance to her hotel.

"This is where I get off," she said.

The Angleterre had been the British Embassy during the American Revolution. Hemingway had stayed there. Charles Lindbergh stayed there the night he completed his flight across the Atlantic. It too had been renovated a number of times, with a concurrent erosion of charm on each occasion. But it was still better than most. We'd been talking about almost anything except what each of us was thinking and feeling during the walk. I screwed up my courage for one personal question.

"I can't help it," I said. "*Are* you seeing anyone?"

She smiled and looked into my eyes.

"There's someone I care about. It's a complicated story. But, no, I'm not seeing him in the way you mean."

"Then when can I see you again?"

This seemed to please her.

"Time-wise things are a mess right now," she said. "I'm giving a lecture at a conference in the morning till lunch—that's why I'm here—then I return to Madrid on the night train to be with my mother for a few more days before flying back to Boston. I went through hell getting MIT to give me time off in the middle of classes so soon after spring break."

"So, you've no time at all?"

"I'll have a few hours before my train leaves. I was going to see Consuelo again, but I can change that."

"Would you?"

"Sure."

"Could I come to the lecture?"

She laughed.

"You'll find it very dull, I fear—difficult, but not in an interesting way for you."

I expected she was correct. At dinner I'd exhausted the extent of my knowledge about her proteins and I had little doubt that the papers to be read, including hers, would be way beyond my capacity to interpret. What she didn't know, what she was not prepared to recognize aloud that first night four hours after meeting me, was that my desire to attend her talk derived from the fact that I was falling for her.

"Even so," I said.

"I'll email you the details tonight."

I wanted to kiss her, but I was too nervous to ask. So I just gave her a short bow, bid her goodnight, and watched her enter the hotel.

## 10

By the time I got back to the apartment Carmen had sent me the information about her lecture and thanked me for walking with her. The note was a bit formal, but I was glad to have it. I looked her up online and read as much as I could about her. She'd been teaching and doing research at MIT for many years, garnering numerous grants and prizes. After taking a bath I sent her a goodnight message that wasn't returned and then got into bed with a glass of Muscat de Beaumes de Venise, opened my laptop, and read more of the trial.

> **John Cupperman, MD:** "I saw the body again at St. Michael's Cemetery on the twelfth day of June. At that time, I made a further examination of it. At the original autopsy I had not opened the head. We had the body exhumed and I removed the scalp and opened the head and examined the brain and found conditions negative. There was no fracture of the skull. I did not find any condition of the brain varying in any degree from the normal. At both examinations I made of this child I found no evidence at all of death caused by any fall or blow on the head such as could have been caused by a fall on a hard floor."

What was the deal with these ghoulish *in situ* autopsies? Why, on both occasions, were the autopsies not performed at a hospital? Why was it so difficult to transport her body to a city morgue or health center? Was it a financial thing? Was it a class thing? Would the autopsy of a rich person's child have been performed on the floor of the little girl's bedroom and then later next to her grave at a cemetery?

**"I am James Kelly.** I am a policeman. In June 1916 I was attached to Precinct 66. I got the clothes of the child from her father. I did not see him wrap them up. I got a bundle. It was wrapped in wrapping paper. It was tied with a cord. I took it to the station house and delivered it unopened to Lieutenant McCormick."

John Carroll: "I am a policeman. I received a bundle from Lt. McCormick about five days after the death of the child. I took it to the Clerk of the District Attorney's office. Between the time I received it and delivered it I did not make any change in it. I did not take it to the DA that night. I put it in the basement, in the corner. There was nothing else kept there. Just coal. Nothing else. The following morning, I took the bundle from my home to the station house. I delivered them to William Masterson, the man sitting over there."

William H. Masterson: "I am a process server in the DA's office of this county. I received the bundle from Mr. Carroll. I did not open the bundle while it was on file or make any change in it. The exhibits are under lock and key. Mr. Barry took the bundle from the property clerk's room."

James D. Barry: "I delivered the package to Theron R. Jameson and Captain Morrison. I made no change to the package."

**Theron R. Jameson:** "I am a deputy assistant attorney of this county. I examined the clothing contained in file No. 1191. I went over each and every article carefully. It was wrapped in my presence after I had examined it. Then I went to Dr. Ewing with Captain Morrison. I can't recall how long after. It was not the same day. I have so many of those things to do that I can't state the time. Between the time I made the examination and had them wrapped up again and the time I took them to Dr. Ewing with Captain Morrison, the clothes were locked up in the property room. I left them with the person in charge."

**I am James Ewing:** "I am a pathologist. 'Pathology' refers to the science of disease and the causes and effects of disease on the body, the study of that branch of medicine. My work familiarizes me with the structures of the human body. It is part of my duty as a pathologist to examine microscopically and otherwise all parts of the human body, and to become familiar with their structure. I examined all the articles with the naked eye and picked out two which seemed to contain substances suspicious of semen. One was an undergarment, another was a linen garment. I shall call these an undershirt and a pair of drawers. Under the microscope I discovered spermatozoa. I picked out a spot to work on because it had a rather stiff, starchy appearance, both on the undershirt and on the drawers at the junction of the two legs of the drawers, near what you might call the crotch."

\*\*\*

This was enough to almost guarantee more nightmares. I shut my laptop and put it aside. I felt there was something fishy about what

I was reading. What with all of the medical, police, and county attorney's examination of "the bundle" before the clothing reached the pathologist, you would have thought someone would have noticed the two areas of dried sperm as well. But no. Not a word.

## 11

The Institut Biologie Paris-Seine is on the campus of the Université Pierre et Marie Curie, on the quay Saint Bernard, virtually across the way from my place. I found a seat toward the rear of the lecture hall. Carmen was addressing a large crowd composed of mostly French professors and students. She wore another dress, a blue and white print, and a pair of black canvas platforms. She looked very cool, a very chic structural biologist. Her hair was pulled back into a ponytail and she had reading glasses on for the occasion. If she noticed me, she gave no hint of it.

The paper started off simply enough but then accelerated and left me behind. Rather than continue to try to grasp fragments bearing some relation to my second language, I unplugged and observed the scene. She spoke in perfect French. The other people listening were intently focused and understood the jargon. For me it was mind-boggling how some twenty amino acids conjoined to form proteins, and then how those proteins folded themselves so faithfully, time and again, to construct an enzyme or a cell membrane. It was almost too wondrous for me to try to fathom how they mediated the cells' activities, how cells formed distinctive tissues, and how evolution had painstakingly programmed cell construction and growth into DNA. To wake up and go about one's business each day while holding on to the implications of what she devoted her intellectual life to was overwhelming. I considered the probable accuracy of Dirk's disregard for my own field. It took me the rest of her paper to resuscitate my injured spirit and come to a more balanced conclusion, that what makes a work of art compelling might be almost equally interesting and worthwhile.

The conference wrapped with a small reception. The flirtations of the night before were one thing, but seeing her in the light of day with so many brainy strangers milling about was something else. She finally saw me and walked over.

"You're here."

"You were terrific," I said. "I've little idea what you were talking about, but the crowd was riveted."

We looked at each other as if for a first time, without the protection of darkness, the Seine, or alcohol. Underneath her sense of style and her professional mien I noticed a sadness in her eyes. It made me want to know more about her life. She looked somehow both younger and older than she had the night before.

"Are you free for lunch?" I asked.

"Yes. It will give me the perfect excuse to get out of here. I just need to thank some people first."

"Take your time," I said. "I'll wait for you out in the hall."

I felt like a teenager, which was not a bad way to feel at that point in my life. The other scientists and doctors there had that French thing going for them: a particular kind of thinness and style, the eyeglasses just so, the foulards draped about the neck, a dignified way of standing. There were a lot of unattractive square-toed shoes on the men, but not a single item of athletic clothing. It could not have been more different from the chunky, gluten-free Patagonia-clad crowd that would have attended a similar event at institutions I was familiar with in New England. I waited in the entrance hall, perusing a chaotic array of flyers, tacked to a large bulletin board, for other inscrutable lectures. I checked my phone the way everyone does now, sitting on a marble bench while luxuriating in the feeling of waiting for someone I was attracted to and who I was about to take to lunch for the first time.

She emerged walking fast and wearing sunglasses. I stood and pushed open the heavy doors for her and out we went.

"I have a driver," I confessed. "I hope you don't mind. I wanted to take you to the Brasserie Balzar and it's a bit tricky to get to from here, and the whole Paris taxi thing drives me nuts."

"I don't mind at all. I'm not a Metro person."

I guided her toward a corner.

"He's around the block here."

It was a service I used for airport runs and getting around town now and then, especially at night after boozy dinners in distant arrondissements. The cars were always new Mercedes sedans with blackened windows and the drivers wore charcoal gray suits, white shirts, and black ties, and had an ex-military look to them. Thierry, the guy I always asked for and trusted with my life, held the door for us and off we went.

"You were just great," I said to Carmen.

She looked at me with disbelief and smiled.

"How could you even tell?"

"The poise, the body language, your American-style freshness at the end. I didn't need to understand it, though I'd like to."

"It isn't that hard when you get into it. It just seems that way from the outside."

"I thought, if you were interested, we might do a bit of tit for tat, that after lunch we could go to the Louvre and I could show you the Géricault painting I'm writing about."

"I would love that," she said, looking out her window at the Ile across the way. "I always promise myself I'll go to museums and then I never do."

41

We squeezed into a narrow table in the thick of the brasserie. The place was full as usual with its crowd of Sorbonne professors, some with pretty students male and female, stylish women of a certain age with small dogs, and French visitors from the provinces. We were the only two foreigners, and I was pleased when the maître greeted me by name. We ordered a simple white Côte de Rhône and I sensed neither of us was going to be able to eat very much. She fiddled with the coaster under her glass of wine and rearranged the silverware around her plate. Again, the sadness in her eyes.

"Please don't take this the wrong way," I said, "like in a creepy way, but how would you feel if I came to Madrid?"

"Madrid."

"I know you've only two days there and that you've got to spend time with your mother, but I'd be happy to get myself there and if you had time for a meal or two it might be fun."

"Hmm, I don't know. That might be nice."

"I don't mean to be pushy. It's just a bit frustrating."

"No. I know what you mean. I'm just not used to it. And we hardly know each other."

"That's what I'd like to change," I said. "I'm just being frank with you. Otherwise you'll get on a train this evening and then you're back at MIT and what? Emailing and texting and the occasional call until I get back there. I mean, I'd like to think that might happen anyway, but why not take advantage of the little time we could have right now?"

I was talking too much and probably coming on too strong. I sensed she was flattered but understandably wary.

"I'm sorry," I said again. "I'm getting way ahead of myself."

"No. I get it. It's a nice idea. I just need a bit of time to process it. I mean I may not have any free time at all in Madrid and I'd hate to disappoint you."

42

"Of course. Not to worry. Think about it."

I took her to see *The Raft of the Medusa* and told her the story of the shipwreck it was based on, the French frigate that ran aground in the middle of the sea off Mauritania in 1816, the small horde of passengers that foundered on a raft built from the wreckage, the deaths, the cannibalism, the scandal it led to back in France. I described for her the obsessive way the twenty-seven-year-old Géricault had gone about studying body parts, visiting hospitals and morgues, how he used naked male models that included Delacroix, the love affair he had with his aunt. I tried to be as conversational and un-professorial as possible. She seemed to enjoy it. We left the museum around four. I was exhausted.

"I need to get back to my hotel," she said, "to pick up my bag and all that."

"Where does your train leave from?"

"Austerlitz."

"Have you already packed?"

"Yes. I checked out this morning. My luggage is at reception."

"Why don't I send Thierry for it and you and I can walk back to my place. It's a good spot to wait from. The station is close by. You can rest there and have some tea, make calls, send me away if you want. Ask Consuelo over. Whatever you wish."

She laughed and then considered it.

"Okay. That's very kind of you."

We strolled over to the Quai des Tulleries and then crossed the Pont Neuf onto the Ile de la Cité. From there we made our way to the Ile Saint-Louis. The sun was shining, and it was good to get some exercise and fresh air.

"Can I ask you an impertinent question?" she said.

"Sure."

"Consuelo, and Dirk, mentioned that you have, like, a vast fortune. I looked you up on *Forbes* and I know it's true. And yet you teach art history. How does that work?"

"It works pretty well," I said, not displeased that she had looked me up. "I have to do something with my time. I'm not the kind of creative person I'd like to be. I can't write or paint very well. I've zero interest in business. I love art and I enjoy trying to get young people to love it as well. I've become sort of a one-man band in my tiny academic world, trying to get people to talk about art in the vernacular, avoiding the deadening vocabulary of theory."

"You must have enemies on campus then," she said.

"I had a few at the Institute of Fine Arts in New York, but not at the Clark or at Williams. And I didn't earn my 'vast fortune,' it just fell into my lap. I'll tell you the story if you'd like."

"Only if you want to."

We were just turning onto the Quai d'Orléans.

"My family were lace curtain Irish Catholics from the South Bronx," I said, not knowing why I started there. Fallout from the dream, I expect. "Mostly men in the liquor business and in law and politics who did all right for themselves and their freckled housewives. I attended a strict Catholic elementary school and grew up during the school year in a middling to lower class neighborhood. But my mother's father was well connected so we summered in Southampton, Long Island, where we were members of the fancy Beach Club."

"I've heard of it."

"So I was a bit of an outsider in both those environments. My mother died when I was very young and my father remarried when I was thirteen, married another Irish Catholic, but this one had a lot of money. At that point we moved from the Bronx to Manhattan. Anyway, I met Scarlett, my wife, at the Beach Club in my teens. She and her parents were recent members. They were from Texas. Her grandfather had something to do with Howard Hughes, helped him invent the drill bit that the Hughes fortune came from, and then he went on to acquire scads of oil fields that he later sold to the Standard Oil Company of New York for an ungodly sum. These were real huntin'-shootin' Texans, but in the case of Scarlett and her mother, Texans who'd gone to finishing schools."

"Scarlett? That was her real name?"

"That was her real name. In the Waspy New England world of the Beach Club she was an outsider too, and I think that was what brought us together. When we were fifteen, she was reading William Burroughs, James Baldwin, and Djuna Barnes, and I was going on in the most pretentious way imaginable about Pollock, Rothko, and the Lascaux cave paintings. Normal-ish activity for teens living in the Village perhaps, but absolutely alien out on Long Island."

We reached the Pont de la Tournelle and kept on going.

"Anyhow," I continued, "in our early twenties she and I lost touch. After college I bummed around Europe pretending to be a painter and she married a very sweet, very rich, fucked-up older gay guy called Bunky Bass, who she truly loved. Both of them had alcoholic parents and they made a pact to keep each other's backs. They set up house in New York mostly, in the 'palazzo' Dirk referred to last night. They each saw people on the side but that never got in the way of the security the marriage provided. I've no idea what kind of sex, if any, went on between them, but they had no kids."

"You never asked?"

"I never asked. They went to church on Sundays. They were fun but also drank a lot and were famous for their liquor-soaked parties. Should I stop? Is this too much information?"

"Don't you dare."

"I ran into her again in New York when I was finishing my degree at the Institute of Fine Arts. This was before I started teaching there. We met for drinks at Bemelman's Bar a few times and started seeing each other in an apartment she kept at the Carlyle."

"Give me a break," she said.

Once again, I feared she was judging me as a superficial one-percenter. I rushed to finish.

"When Bunky died of AIDS she was devastated and asked me to marry her, which I did. We were both thirty-five years old. I was looking to settle down and she wanted to somehow maintain the safe feeling that her marriage to Bunky gave her."

"What was she like?"

"She was complicated, pretty, loved to ride. She wasn't an intellectual, but she did read all the time, literature mostly. She was selfish in some ways, vain, insecure, prone to addiction, but very sweet underneath it all—and very loyal to me."

"So, what happened?"

"The drinking and the pills got worse. She refused to do anything about it. It got to be unbearable and after a while I started being unfaithful to her. She knew. She didn't correspond in kind. Her emotionally abusive father, who she adored, had done the same thing with her mother. Anyway, in the end, it lasted some twenty years, until she died going on five years ago."

"Twenty years," she said. "That's a long time."

"A lifetime. I cared for her very much. It's strange—my mother, who drank very little, died of liver cancer, and Scarlett, who drank like a fish and never smoked, died of lung cancer."

"So the fortune Dirk and Consuelo can't stop talking about comes from her."

"That's right. Her fortune and Bunky's fortune combined."

"You sort of did what your father did, marrying into money."

"That's right," I said again. "It was one of the few things we had in common."

"And since then?"

"You mean relationships?"

"Yes."

"Some more serious than others, but none that have lasted."

"Why is that, do you think?"

"I don't run into that many people," I said. "I mostly live between Lenox and Williamstown."

"But—not to fuel your ego—you're an attractive man, and you're rich, you must be pursued all the time."

"Not really. I mean, thanks to some early mistakes I've gotten pretty good at recognizing various kinds of gold-diggers. And I live modestly, compared with how I could. I'm not out there on display, as it were. And I've been lucky. I like what I do. I have a bunch of trustworthy lawyers and accountants who take care of bills and taxes and handle my philanthropy each year to assuage my conscience. I live pretty simply, relatively speaking. I look around and see others in my situation or in my bracket or however you want to call it, who lead complicated, stressful lives with lots of staff and assistants. People who have trouble sitting still."

She flashed a grin. "What makes you think I'm not a gold-digger?"

"I can tell you aren't."

"I *guess* that's a compliment."

"It is."

"Maybe you're not as perceptive as you think."

I paused and we leaned against the parapet by the river.

"My story's a bit different," she said. "My ex-husband is still alive, for one, and except for the very beginning we never got on very well and it only lasted half of what yours did. I've become fairly cynical about 'relationships.'"

"In what sense?"

"We're born based on other people's whims, needs, or mistakes, and we die alone. Who we bump into in between is pretty much ruled by chance. Yet just about every song and love poem I know insists on the hand of fate, something that was *meant to be*. But looking at it objectively . . ."

"As a biologist."

"As a biologist, I don't buy it."

"Where did fate decree that you two meet?"

"At Oxford. I worked there for a time, doing research."

"He's British."

"A British psychoanalyst, considerably older than me, like you. He had a practice in London, a few patients at the College, and a country house in the Cotswolds."

"That sounds very nice."

"Right? I thought so too. I think I fell more in love with the situation than I did with him."

"It got rocky."

"It got rocky quickly. It was a mistake to have gotten married at all, really. I know it's a bit of a cliché but so many analysts I've met, including Matthew and his colleagues, are mad as hatters."

"How do you get on with him now?"

"Not well. I'm the one who left, and so even now, over a year later, he alternates between fits of anger and declarations of unrequited love, neither of which I care to deal with."

"And no kids."

"Thank god. He had two from his first marriage, who are quite grown up. I don't really think I can have them anyway, physically I mean."

"Me either."

"Really."

"Sub-zero sperm count. Inherited from my mother's side. It has a name I can't remember."

"I'm sorry. Have you missed being a father?"

"Occasionally. Though I'm not a great fan of children. I'm not one of those people who find them automatically adorable. Not having them has freed my life up considerably."

She looked away. It might not have been the smartest thing to say.

"And your folks?" I asked, eager to change the subject. "Are they still alive?"

"My father died some years ago. My mother lives in Madrid."

"Right. Duh. Of course."

## 12

The lobby of my building, a very old hôtel particulier, and then the apartment came to the rescue.

"Oh my god," she said, walking into the entrance hall, raising her hands to her mouth.

"You like it?"

"How could you live anywhere else?"

"I'm not sure what I'd do here all year round. I like my neck of the woods in Massachusetts too. I'm grateful to the Clark for letting me organize a special exhibition now and then, and I have my students."

I took her coat.

"I got this place on my own, by the way," I added. "After Scarlett died."

We walked into the living room.

"It's extraordinary," she said, looking around.

"Baudelaire lived here once upon a time. I had to do a serious renovation, new plumbing and wiring, new bathrooms and kitchen. But otherwise it's pretty much as it was."

"And the furniture?"

"Some of it was here. The rest I've acquired over the years."

"On your own?"

"I hate decorators."

She went over to the line of tall windows that opened in pairs looking down at the Seine.

"Well, it's just divine."

"I toyed with the idea of going minimalist, very white, and cleaning it out. But in the end, I went with the sort of place I imagine the Impressionists living in. Cozy but not cluttered. Comfortable furniture, big comfy beds, lots of flowers, paintings, mirrors."

After finishing the tour, we ended up in the kitchen where I made us some tea. Thierry phoned to say he had her bags and I told him to take a few hours off and be back in time to take her to the station.

Had it been a film, a European film, the situation by then would have clamored for a seduction scene. The time constraint and the approaching train whistle begged for an act of passion *a l'apres midi*. But we were still getting to know each other, and I was happy just listening to her talk. So we returned to the living room and leaned over the balconies and watched the Bateaux Mouches pass by. Then she turned to me and said, out of the blue, "You've never been in love, have you."

I was silent for a moment, considering it. "No," I said. "I agree. I have not." Her eyes went tender then and sparkled with intelligence. I felt an overwhelming desire to tell her about my dream. I had a hunch she would understand it.

And so I did. I described it in detail and included the day remnants preceding it, including the anniversaries of my mother's and my wife's deaths.

"I think it's pretty obvious the date is what set things off," she said. "Right?"

"And you must have heard *some*thing about this case when you were little. No? Otherwise it's just too weird."

"My father's parents are the best candidates. They had to know these people. It happened in their basement."

"Or maybe your father told you."

A barge went by. The wash and chugging noise always pleased me. A snobby, resentful acquaintance of mine considered the barges and the tour boats the great disadvantage of living on a quay of the Ile. I loved them.

I told Carmen how my father had talked to me in bed a lot during the year after my mother died. How I slept in the bed that had been hers. It was pushed up next to his. He'd get home tipsy late at night and wake me. What I most remembered was him telling me what a good man the Judge was. I later thought he said it so often because he felt guilty about not taking better care of me. On her deathbed my mother made the Judge promise to look after me. So perhaps there was something about my father she didn't entirely trust. These memories of him were ones I cherished. The closeness of him. His simple sincerity. The white T-shirts and boxer shorts from De Pinna. The way the booze washed away his lawyerly authority, revealing a man at sea.

"And you say he and the Swedish girl were the same age," she said.

"They must have known each other," I said, "played together. It must have been traumatic for him and the other children who lived in that building and on that block."

She went over to the fireplace. I fantasized we already lived there together and then worried this might be the kind of moment I would someday take for granted, become inured to, that I would lose the capacity to appreciate the grace of her movements, the way she held her teacup and tilted her head.

"If I was told about it and I've repressed it all this time," I said, "I just wonder why it's percolated to the surface now, regardless of the date."

She looked at me.

"I don't know you well enough to know."

"Of course not."

"I mean we don't know each other at all, really."

There she was saying it again.

"And yet I feel I've known you for a long time," I said. "I'm sorry if that sounds corny, but there you have it."

"It sounds like you may be making an argument for fate," she said.

"Fate, no," I said, lying. "Luck, maybe."

"Maybe you overheard things, but assuming somebody did tell you about this little girl," she said, "what do you think they might have said? What would have been the moral of the tale?"

"Sadism?"

She laughed.

"Not to talk with strangers?" I said.

"That sounds more like it. Maybe it was the first time you were forced to think about death."

"Oh, I'd already thought about death. When my mother first got sick, they thought she was pregnant. It's what they told me. The thought that a new baby was on its way to hijack the love she rained down on me was untenable. I wanted it dead. I wanted it gone. And then I got my wish. But I didn't want my mother to die. All of my life since then I've been terrified of being found out, of having my crime revealed. I've been hounded inside by a great fear of being caught."

"You mentioned Anne Frank."

"Yes. The scene, the sequence, when she and her family are discovered and arrested, terrified me."

"So the siren you heard before falling asleep that night got that association going."

"Without a doubt."

"You cut the wire binding your legs together and then ran, frightened of being apprehended."

"That's how it went."

"But then you mentioned the Abraham and Isaac reference, in which a father is prepared to murder his own son. I'm not sure I get the connection."

"It's something to do with sacrifice. The Ingrid murder, reading about it, I'm getting a sacrificial vibe."

"Or maybe you have some issues about children."

"I hadn't thought of that. Hey, would you like a little champagne?"

She laughed again. "Why not?"

When I came back with it, she was looking at the river again. She turned my way.

"The dream is really interesting," she said.

"Where is your ex-husband when we need him?"

"You know," she said, "he wears those same round glasses the Ed Wynn character in your dream did. But I'm sure you can figure this out without him."

"You should read the transcript from the trial," I said, peeling the metallic foil off the top of the bottle. "It's very compelling, though hard to take at times."

"I'd like to."

"I'll email you a copy."

I popped the cork and filled our glasses.

When it was time for her to go, Thierry held the car door open and I kissed her on both cheeks. I watched them pull away until the Mercedes made its turn onto the Pont de Sully, in the hope she might turn around and wave a final time. But she didn't.

The last exchange we had on the street was, "So what about Madrid?"

"Oh, right," she said. "Well, come if you can. That would be great. I'm sure I'll find a way for us to see each other."

"Good. I've been meaning to visit the Prado Museum for a while now anyway. I'll text you when I get there and if you've got some time we can continue the conversation."

I made the last flight to Madrid that evening. A taxi got me to the Ritz in time for a late dinner. Not interested in hotel food, I took the concierge's suggestion and found my way to a small Navarran bistro within walking distance, near to what had been the city's main post office and that was now the town hall. Invigorated by the sudden journey and change of culture, I sat at the bar and ordered some wine, Serrano ham, and fried artichoke hearts. It was close to midnight and the place was still jumping with people seated at tables finishing their meal or having after-dinner drinks. I walked back to the hotel wishing I had spent more time in that city. My room—the hotel had recently been renovated from head to toe—was large and pleasantly appointed and looked across at the Prado. After a hot bath I got into bed, set my alarm, and read a bit more from the trial. I decided not to contact Carmen until the next day.

## 13

**Catherine Moriarty:** "I reside at 1075 Ogden Avenue. I am fifteen years old. I knew Ingrid Anderson who lived in that house. I remember the day her body was found in the cellar. I know the defendant MacBride by sight. On that afternoon I was playing stoop ball at 1077. We were catching it against the stoop. I was playing with all the children around there. I did not see the defendant while playing there. I saw him that afternoon sitting on the stone wall. We were playing until about a half past six. I don't remember how long I saw him there. The wall is about a half block from where we were playing. Ingrid was sitting on the stoop of 1077. She stayed there all the time we were playing and when I went home she was still there. I am positive, because I remember I asked her if she was not going up for her supper, and she said no. I never saw Ingrid alive again."

**Arthur Woolf:** "I am ten and a half years old. I reside at 1077 Ogden Avenue. I knew Ingrid Anderson. I did not play with her much. I play with boys. She lives next door. I know MacBride by sight. I remember the day Ingrid was found in the cellar. I was playing with Ingrid and her brother Edwin. I saw MacBride while I was playing there. I heard Ingrid say, 'Give me a penny.' I don't know who she meant it for. I don't know whether she meant it for MacBride or for me. MacBride was on the stoop at the time. We were playing where the two houses are attached. She looked at MacBride when she said it. He did not say anything to her. After we stopped playing my mother took me up in the house to eat my supper. Ingrid stayed there on the stoop. When I went up in the house MacBride was not there. I know Mr. Conlan. I know MacBride lived with Conlan."

**Rita Moriarty:** "I am twelve years old. I am the sister of Catherine Moriarty. I knew Ingrid Anderson. I remember the day she died. I did not see her that day. I saw her two days before. I saw Ingrid get a penny from MacBride.

**Francis Buckley:** "I am twelve years old and reside at 1075 Ogden Avenue. I remember the day Ingrid was found in the cellar. We were playing stoop ball. Ingrid was on the stoop of 1075. I was playing with the Colossi boy. I did not see Catherine Moriarty there. I saw Arthur Woolf on the other stoop with Ingrid and her brother Edwin. The two houses are right next to each other. MacBride was standing on the top of the stoop of 1077 while we were playing. We hit him with the ball by accident. He told us to throw the ball down lower and after that he came down the stairs and went away. I saw him walk in the direction of the firehouse just across the way. When I left I did not see MacBride around anywhere. He did not come back to the house again while I was there."

**Bernard Carl Valiunas:** "I am a saloon keeper opposite 1075 and 1077 Ogden Avenue, next to the firehouse. I know MacBride. I remember the night when the child was found. I saw and heard the ambulance come. I stood outside the place.

When the ambulance came, I saw MacBride. He was alongside the firehouse. He stayed there a couple of minutes and then came into my place in an ordinary way and asked me for a drink of whiskey. He was in a hurry. More people came in and he went out. I have known him for four or five years. I did not notice anything odd about him when he was drinking."

***

I stopped reading here. The parents, the Andersons, referred to their son as Adranaxa. But the Woolf child and the Francis Buckley kid called him Edwin. I wondered why everyone in the transcript was referred to by their full names, or by their title, all except for the defendant, whom everyone simply called "MacBride."

The children's testimonies sounded coached to me. My father and brothers, all of whom lived at 1077 Ogden Avenue, did not appear in the transcript. Why? School was in session on the sixth of June. Surely they were there. And where were my grandparents? Wasn't Pop Kerry also in Bernard Carl Valiunas's saloon, or part of the crowd gathered about the ambulance? The Colossi child was surely my very own Gino, the namesake of the miserly barber up the street, Francis Buckley's little friend who grew up to be my father's driver, the man who often slept at our house, who cut our hair on the lawn in Southampton, who drove me into Manhattan in his cigar-smelling Chrysler. The timeline was confusing. Last seen at six-thirty and found at ten, when had Ingrid Anderson been raped and strangled to death? Whose sperm was it that had stained her garments?

The more I thought about it the more I was convinced that in that pre-DNA-testing world, poor MacBride had been framed. He came across to me like the Boo Radley of the neighborhood, easy pickings for cops who were suspiciously eager to solve the case quickly. Were the police in on it in some macabre way? Or maybe, because the victims were immigrants, they didn't really give a damn. Who might have been the rapist and murderer capable of squeezing his hands about the little girl's throat with all their might, for three long minutes, in the basement of the house where she and so many people lived? Had the rape occurred before or after he killed her?

Stoop ball. The children had been playing stoop ball. I had played it too, against the very same stoop, four decades later. It raised the hairs on the back of my neck.

## 14

The next morning I had breakfast in the dining room and texted Carmen to let her know I was there. She answered right away.

*Where are you staying?*

*The Ritz.*

*Of course. Might we have dinner tomorrow evening?*

*Yes.*

*Nine-ish?*

*Perfect. I'll reserve. I look forward to it.*

The day and evening yawning open before me presented a stretch of time that felt interminable. I went out and walked around the immediate neighborhood until the Spanish lunch hour. Not being a fan of that substantial Iberian meal, I went to the Prado when most people in Madrid, or so I thought, would be tucking in. But the museum was filled with tourists. I wandered from hall to hall, walking quickly, only stopping before paintings I have special affection for: Velasquez's *Head of a Deer*, Zurbarán's *Agnus Dei*, Goya's *Dog Half Buried in the Sand*. Along with every other yo-yo and despite my sophisticated professorial credentials, I marveled once again at *Las Meninas*. Finally, spurred on by my interest in the quote that grabbed my attention in Leiris's *L'Age d'homme*, I found Andrea del Sarto's painting, *The Sacrifice of Isaac*.

The story, taken from Genesis, a text written down at least as early as the sixth century BCE, was one that Christian artists like del

Sarto consistently depicted as an allegory for the so-called Passion of Christ. As a twenty-first-century man I could only view these things as stories from primitive times whose intention was to urge moral restraint on human instincts. Though children *were* sacrificed in ancient eras, and though it persisted as a theme in certain satanic rites, what was it really all about?

I had a sandwich and a coffee in the museum cafeteria while reading the *New York Times* on my phone. Almost all of the people around me, Italians, Japanese, Chinese, Northern Europeans, rich Russians, and various species of Americans, had abandoned the notion of leather shoes. The *New York Times*, desperate to keep up with social media sites, was becoming increasingly vacuous, article after article about food and relationships and *problèmes de riches*. I left the museum and walked through the Botanical Gardens where new blossoms were only beginning to appear, then crossed the Castellana and wandered up through the Barrio de las Letras.

I avoided strolling up the Calle de las Huertas, where, if its name bore any relation to its origins, centuries earlier there had once been tilled gardens growing vegetables. Now, free of vehicular traffic, it was lined with bars and awash with people. I went by the cloistered Trinitarias convent under whose central patio Cervantes was said to be buried, where the sister of his rival playwright, Lope de Vega, spent her final years as a nun. I went up the Calle Lope de Vega to the Calle del León, a jolly street with a hipper feel to it, and then walked up the Calle del Prado, lined with antique stores, to the Plaza Santa Ana. This plaza—where the Cerveceria Alemana still exists, a place little changed from when it was patronized by Hemingway, and where the Teatro Español has stood in one form or another since the middle of the eighteenth century—has also been made tourist and family friendly. It was jammed to the gills. The former Hotel Victoria, where so many bullfighters had prepared for and recovered from their strange occupation, was now a very modern hotel, a black napkin sort of place with a disco on the roof. I avoided the city's nearby main square entirely, the Puerta del Sol, the nation's geographic center, the reason why in 1561 Philip II chose Madrid to be the capital of Spain, for it too was blanketed with people. It was dominated by a mammoth Apple store and sprinkled with roaming mimes.

It was only after I had pushed my way through the impressive but garish Plaza Mayor, and made my way down into the labyrinthine, narrow streets of old Madrid, the *Madrid de las Austrias*, that my itinerary rewarded me with an architecture and ambiance that pleased me to no end. Little taverns and restaurants, as inconspicuous as they were promising, graced the winding lanes of weathered stone. A smell of lamb chops on the grill mixed with cooler air. A younger, nicer-looking crowd lived and circulated there, mixing easily with shop owners in their seventies wearing clean aprons, people who kept neat and orderly stores from another time.

I emerged from one of these streets onto the Plaza de la Paja, a beautiful, sloping square surrounded by grand old apartments, a church, small restaurants, and a walled-in garden open to the public that was part of a former palace belonging to someone called the Principe de Anglona. I ended up having a cup of tea at the Café del Oriente, facing the royal palace, cheek by jowl with the national opera house, pleased to be back in a city I had last visited five years earlier, just after Scarlett was buried. Remembering streets and places, comparing what I remembered with what I was seeing that day, provided me with a modicum of satisfaction. It was not a city I knew well, but now that I was identifying it with Carmen, it took on a special resonance.

In the late afternoon I went to the Reina Sofía Museum to contemplate Picasso's *Guernica*. I don't consider it a great work of art, but as a teenager soaking up culture and doing what I could to forge an identity, to show off and to try to talk to girls, I'd spent hours in the Museum of Modern Art in New York. That was where this painting had always been, as far as I was concerned, and where I believed it still belonged. I knew its tale and the historical context that explained its voyage back across the Atlantic to Spain, but all it did for me was bring back those days of being a teenage flaneur in Manhattan, going to the movies at the Paris and Sutton theaters. I would peruse the stacks in the Librairie de France at Rockefeller Center and intentionally bump into other customers just so I could say "*Pardonnez-moi.*" I remembered sharing pieces of an incredibly delicious chocolate cake with a girlfriend at the Women's Exchange on Madison and Fifty-Fifth, where I once saw Cary Grant having cocktails with Fred Astaire. Dancing the twist at Shepherds disco with the Ford sisters and Killer Jo Piro. Throwing up in the men's room at Malkan's. Overdoing a first French kiss at L'Interdit.

My recollections of those afternoons spent in the MOMA were particularly sweet. Its clean lines. The leaves blown along the curb of West Fifty-Fifth Street. The Bell helicopter, Monet's *Water Lilies*, Matisse's *Red Room*, my callow, absurd seriousness. I had fancied myself as Stephen Dedalus, Eugene Gant, Robert Jordan, and the James Dean of *Giant* all rolled into one. I was both Jean-Louis Trintignant and Pierre Barouh in *Un Homme et Une Femme*. I was Belmondo in *Pierre LeFou* and Nino Castelnuovo in *The Umbrellas of Cherbourg*. The *Guernica* that meant so much to so many people with lives so much more tragic and serious than mine was a three-and-a-half-meter-long talisman for me.

I managed to stay out until seven-thirty without being unduly distracted by either Carmen or Ingrid Anderson. Leaving the Reina Sofia and confronted with the ugly plaza in front of it, I stepped into a restaurant named Arzábal next door and sat at the bar, ordering

Jamón Serrano and a good, cold white wine from Valdeorras. Some sort of event was going on in a private dining room. Spanish men in suits too tight for them, sporting complicated wristbands, big watches, and holding on to cell phones, came and went snatching canapés off silver trays. I wondered what Carmen might be up to, walked back to the Ritz, and read another bit of testimony before falling asleep.

\*\*\*

**Alexander J. Conlan:** "I reside at 1059 Ogden Avenue. I am the brother-in-law of the defendant. I was living with his sister in June 1916, at 1077 Ogden Avenue. The defendant was living with me there that day, June 6, 1916. I left the house at about half past seven that morning and returned after two in the afternoon. When I came back, he was standing in the doorway of my office and the first thing I asked him was, had there been any customers. He said no there had not. I called him into the shop and I said, 'Gene, you have either got to get work or you will have to find some other quarters.' I could not afford to keep him with us at the apartment without some return for his board, and he got kind of uppish about it, and I said, 'Get work or get out; and the quicker you get out the better.' I went home again. I was wringing wet. It had been raining very heavily that morning and I went home to change clothes and have some lunch. My wife asked me to have Gene bring up some kindling wood. I told Gene to bring up some kindling wood and some meat I had bought in the butcher shop. I next saw Gene about a little after four o'clock, he had just come back from the house to the shop. I said, 'Did you bring up the meat?' And he said yes, he had just come back.

"After that we were both in the shop, here and there, in and out, up to about six or six thirty. Then we both took an armful of wood. We went home for supper. It was not quite ready, and we sat around the house until about seven o'clock. I left him there. He did not appear in any way excited. He appeared just like he always is. I saw him again in the neighborhood around eight o'clock standing on the steps leading to my stoop. That is where the stone wall is up there that there is so much talk about. I did not talk to him at the time. I was on the opposite side of the street. Then I saw him off and on until the time of the excitement over this little girl being found. At the time they found her I saw him in the cellar where there were quite a lot of people, men and women. I didn't go upstairs until about three o'clock in the morning. I waited until after the coroner left. The last time I saw Gene that evening was about eleven thirty and he went upstairs at that time. The next time I saw him was on Saturday, the eighth of June, in New Rochelle.

"I am not living with my wife now. We broke up on account of money matters. I didn't have enough money to pay the rent. When the officer asked me where MacBride was the night of June sixth I told him that MacBride had spent the night and that I had last seen him at eleven thirty. When MacBride was in the house, I generally slept in my own bed in the front room right off the parlor. Quite often I slept with MacBride in the room there. The flat has five rooms. The bedroom where my wife and the children were sleeping leads off the parlor. The dining room is right next to the parlor. The mattress in the parlor was an extra mattress that we had. It was standing in the corner on the floor. There was one blanket on it. I had a bed right in the next room, all made up. I did not sleep in the bedroom off the parlor that night. I slept in the parlor. I just felt that way about it. It happened quite often that I didn't occupy my room. I went in about three o'clock in the morning and there were no lights lit or anything, and there was that mattress standing in the corner of the parlor. I spread it on the floor, undressed myself and laid on it. The only reason why I took the trouble to lay out a mattress on the floor in the parlor instead of going into my own room was because I felt that way. My wife did not tell me that MacBride said he was going away. She told me that he had said for her to set the clock at six in the morning for him. I don't know when he left."

# – 15 –

Breakfast in my room. Good tea. Delicious toast. Terrible croissants. The *New York Times* crossword completed with a minimum of cheating. iPhone news browsing. Shower.

All that got me to eleven-thirty. I was on my way to the Prado again to buy and ship some books home to Lenox when I got a new text message from Carmen.

*Awake?*

*Good morning.*

*Where are you?*

*On my way to the Prado bookstore.*

*Are we on for tonight?*

*Of course. Horcher at 9:15. Do you know it?*

*A classic!*

*Like me.*

*Expensive.*

*My treat.*

*What about lunch?*

*"In addition to" I hope.*

*Yes. My treat.*

Following instructions, I found her two hours later at a municipal market smack in the middle of the fancy part of town, the Mercado de la Paz in the Barrio Salamanca. The market was relatively small and filled with an appealing mix of food stalls and places to eat. Fruit, fish, meat and fowl, vegetables, bread, wine and cheese vendors, hardware, dry cleaning, and three or four simple restaurants. The people who worked there, a blend of hearty no-nonsense Madrileños and sharp Hispanic immigrants, contrasted with the clientele, conservative and wealthy by and large, the women more attractive than the men. Many of the latter were in peacock mode; tight jeans, suede shoes with orange or red laces, and tight blue or green jackets with fake elbow patches. The slicked-back hair ending in small curls look persisted here. A foppish mix of Austrian hunting attire and Euro preppy-ism prevailed.

Carmen was easy to find. In jeans and a short leather jacket, her hair pulled back, revealing small gold hoop earrings, I was once again smitten with this very beautiful MIT structural biologist, entirely at home in this quintessential Madrid setting. She carried numerous plastic bags of food. She smiled. We exchanged kisses on both cheeks.

"You found it."

"GPS."

"Very crafty. I thought I'd show you how the other half has lunch here. Cheap and authentic, though somewhat chaotic."

I relieved her of two of her bags.

"I'm in your hands."

It was called Casa Dani. It was chaotic because it was extremely popular. From what I could tell, it had at least three entrances. A long bar was filled with people already eating. The main dining area had walls of sliding glass that permitted views of the market. She knew where the most responsive line formed and how to deal with the sweating pre-heart-attack waiter who was more or less in charge of assigning tables. New customers and waiters and waitresses were squeezing through the narrow spaces between the many tables jammed with patrons from all walks of life. Workers in blue overalls stained with paint and cement dust sat alongside executives in Brioni suits with Hermes ties. The pace was frantic, the noise deafening; clattering plates brusquely set down and collected, orders hollered over multiple animated conversations.

The food was delicious. At eleven euros a head, including a no-nonsense wine and dessert, the total for the both of us was one-third of what they charged at the Ritz for my solitary breakfast. Carmen ordered broccoli and I a rice stew with bits of lobster in it for starters. Then she had a Dorada fish grilled to perfection and I had some juicy roast chicken accompanied by homemade French fries. We drank water in lieu of wine and both of us had fresh strawberries floating in a little puddle of freshly squeezed orange juice for dessert along with decaf espressos. It was hard to hear oneself during the meal, for the place remained amazingly crowded throughout, but it was great fun. The only other tourists I noticed willing to wait on the line and put up with the hullabaloo were, of course, French.

"This is extraordinary," I said, practically screaming.

"I'm glad you like it. You've passed a test. I was afraid you might stick your nose up."

"Not at all," I said, pleased.

"I still don't know how the staff does this every day."

The last lunch we'd shared had been two days earlier at the Brasserie Balzar. It felt like two months had gone by since then.

"I don't suppose you've had a chance to read any of the trial."

"Yes!" she said. "Pages and pages of it on the train. It's fascinating. Gruesome and fascinating."

"Right? I'm about halfway through it."

"What do you think?" she asked, picking carefully with her knife and fork, prying bits of fish from the bone. I imagined her in a lab coat performing tasks with similar care. I widened my eyes as if to ask for clarification.

"Do you think he did it?" she asked.

"No," I said. "I don't."

"I didn't either at first," she said. "But now I'm not so sure."

"He could have. You're right," I said. "But I think he was framed."

"By whom? The cops?"

"By somebody," I said. "If ever there was a case for DNA testing."

"Have you noticed it's all about men?"

"Not really."

"The defendant, the judge, the jury, the lawyers, the cops, and 90 percent of the witnesses," she said, using her fingers to list them.

"I hadn't thought of it. Interesting point. Speaking of men, there's one staring at us through the glass behind you."

She turned and looked.

"Oh my god," she said. "What is he doing here?"

"You know him?"

"Yes. I'm sorry. I have to deal with this."

"Perhaps I should stick around, in case you need anything."

"No," she said. "I'll be fine. He's just someone going through a difficult time."

"All right."

She got up and started gathering her bags.

"I'll take care of lunch," I said.

"It was supposed to be my treat."

"You can treat me some other time."

"Thank you," she said, trying to hide how embarrassed she was.

"If you like I could have your shopping delivered to your mother's," I said. It seemed unfair for her to have to deal with whoever this guy was weighed down with perishable goods. "I fibbed about using GPS to get here. I've got a car and driver waiting out there somewhere. If there's someone to receive it, the driver could bring it to her door."

"Would you?"

"Easy as pie. Just write down the address."

I was glad to be helpful. I handed her a pen and a paper napkin. She wrote it down.

"I'll call you later," she said. And then she was gone.

Handsome and closer to her in age I assumed the fellow was an ex-boyfriend. Though I could understand any man's heartache from being spurned by her, this unsolicited and unexpected appearance was a pain. During the forty-five seconds it took her to extricate herself from the dining area, exit Casa Dani, and walk around to encounter the sulking intruder, he and I glanced at each other a few times through the glass panel.

I waited for them to leave and then waited some more before picking up her bags of food plus one from a store called Bimba & Lola. I paid and walked through the market, most of its stalls closed or closing by then. I paused to watch how carefully one of the seafood vendors cleaned their premises. Wearing rubber aprons and wellies, strong, good-humored men with roots in the north used high-pressure hoses that hung from the ceiling to wash away scales and innards. Large unsold merluzas were carefully repacked into thick Styrofoam containers cushioned with plentiful amounts of fresh ice.

I found the car parked on the Calle de Ayala, the driver enjoying a beer and a *pincho* of tortilla at a bar just next to it. I insisted he finish and then gave him the address and we made our way through the center of Madrid over to its western edge, to an elegant, tree-lined street called the Paseo del Pintor Rosales, across from a park. I waited in the car while the driver delivered her groceries and wondered how it was going with Carmen and the mystery man. I didn't know a damn thing, but I assumed and prayed she had officially ended their relationship, maybe quite recently, and that he was unwilling to accept it and had been following her. I sincerely hoped it would be resolved that afternoon, that it wouldn't cancel or put too burdensome a damper on the evening's dinner with me.

Her mother's building was 1970s modern, eight stories tall with lots of terraces, all of them with flowers in planter boxes and some with potted trees. I wondered if she had lived there as a young girl before she went off to New York, had gone to grade school and even high school nearby, leaving and returning to this building, playing in the park across the way, smoking on the corner, making out with first beaus.

I thought about the Bronx I grew up in. Highbridge back then had been calm, home to a successful working-class population of Irish Catholics and Jews. Though Spain had gone through a horrific civil war around the time Carmen's mother was born, this neighborhood looked as if it hadn't changed much at all in the last fifty years, whereas the Bronx had changed dramatically.

Though I returned to Highbridge in dreams, I was unable to return there physically. It was simply out of the question. I was incapable of it. That the Judge's house, the elegant home where my mother grew up and had her wedding party, the house featured in my dream, that that house had been abandoned and its roof caved in was irrelevant. That the doormen and the stately green awning that ran from the wrought iron filigreed doors to the curb of Undercliff Avenue had disappeared, replaced by a single smudged plexiglass door and a graffiti-smirched aluminum plaque of buzzers was irrelevant as well. Ogden Avenue had evolved from a long, meandering, tranquil road lined with brownstones, saloons, churches, synagogues, cinemas, firehouses, barber shops, and markets into a run-down, semi-abandoned Calvary of half-empty buildings, vacant lots, and bodegas. None of this did anything to penetrate the psychological wall inside me. I knew of these changes thanks to a quick drive-through I did one afternoon returning from upstate New York years ago that later required a bottle of wine to recover from. I had no idea about the real cause of my paralysis. But the expression that most reverberated within me whenever I thought about it was *the scene of the crime.*

Carmen, who'd studied and worked and found a successful way to live far from her original nest—this telling me that she too had undergone difficulty and that she too lived in some ambivalence with respect to her home—was nevertheless able to return here. She enjoyed Madrid and went back to this apartment I sat in front of without, as far as I knew, having to self-medicate to get through it.

My conundrum was very different. Perhaps it was the fact that it had been a real crime that took place in my family's basement, a crime from much longer ago, a crime that was inviting me to attach all manner of feelings and emotions of my own to it without having to face what, apparently, despite decades of therapy and significant introspection, continued to haunt me—my own murder story.

The driver returned. I sent him back to the hotel and decided to take a stroll in the Parque del Oeste, the Western Park. It was in full bloom and replete with joggers, children, skateboarders, and retirees sitting on wooden benches resting their chins on canes. Tall umbrella pines I associated with the countryside around Rome lorded over rose gardens and lawns and well-kept paths and monuments to Spanish wars, writers, and former colonies.

I sat at a café facing the rebuilt Temple of Debod, a beautiful construction from Egypt, 200 BCE. It reminded me of the Temple of Dendur at the Met in New York. Small children were playing near it and I could tell from their bossy voices that their game was being invented right then and there and that they were making up complicated and contradictory rules as they went along, each new rule favoring whichever child spoke it. They were adorable and at the same time rather frightening. I paid for my coffee and moved on, wondering how Carmen was faring. I sent her a message:

*Food delivered. Are you OK?*

No answer. I walked to the Plaza de España and looked at the huge statue of Don Quixote and Sancho Panza and had to raise my hat to a society that placed fictional characters from classic literature in the nation's most central square. A woman walking her dog caught my eye, the dog especially. It was a King Charles spaniel, rapt in a state of high excitement. It was not a puppy; its joy and energy did not derive from inexperience. It was just thrilled to be out and about, sniffing at every leaf, shrub, and water drain within reach, and peeing at the base of the statue. The woman was on her phone and paid it little mind but smiled at me as I leaned down to engage her pet. The smooth feel of its pelt, the cold wetness of its nose, the guileless, slightly bulging eyes looking up into mine affected me with its devotion to the here and now.

In a taxi heading back to the hotel I got a response:

*Thank you for that. All is well. See you this evening.*

## 16

B ack in my suite with a few hours to kill, I flopped down on the bed and read some of MacBride's testimony. As I did, I realized the original trial had taken place before a coroner, that MacBride had been found guilty, and that he had been sentenced to be executed in the electric chair at Sing Sing, the infamous prison on the Hudson River north of the city. The transcript I had was from MacBride's appeal trial. I googled "New York City coroner" and learned that the office had been abolished just a year after MacBride's trial took place. Up until then coroners, two in every borough of the city, had the power to convene grand juries and pass sentence on the accused. The system had been abolished due to a pattern of consistent abuse. New York City coroners throughout the 1900s had only sometimes been physicians; some had been undertakers, some were dentists, some were politicians, and one was a butcher.

**Eugene J. MacBride:** "I am thirty-three years old. I was born in Scotland. I have been living in New York for twenty-eight years. I am not married. In June 1916, I was living at 1077 Ogden Avenue with Alexander J. Conlan, a brother-in-law. He is married to my sister. He lives on the third floor.

"I got up about eleven o'clock in the morning that day, had breakfast and stayed around the house for about an hour. Then I went down to Conlan's shop, about half a block away. Conlan is a plumber. I filled my arms with firewood and brought it up to my sister's home. Then I went down again. There were two boys playing ball on the stoop. One boy I know was the little Buckley boy that was here yesterday and testified about my being struck with the ball.

"I stood on the top step to wait, not wanting to interrupt them from their game, and one of the boys, I don't remember which one it was—threw the ball and it happened to miss the edge of the step, and comes up and hits me in the testicles. That is about the only way I can pronounce that.

"I only said to them, 'Boys, why you ought to be a little bit careful, and play in the lots or go down the street somewhere and play. You will be hurting somebody with your ball. You don't know who might be coming out and it might go in the hall and hit somebody else.' The boys laughed and went on.

"I went over to Barney Valiunas's saloon. That was about four o'clock. I was there until about six thirty. During that time I read the papers and threw dice with Barney. I was sober when I left and in full possession of my faculties. Then I went over for supper and met my brother-in-law at the door. He was in a hurry to meet somebody and finished before I did. I left the house about a quarter after seven, came downstairs and went up to the corner of 165th Street on Ogden Avenue. There I sat on the stone wall in front of my brother-in-law's shop.

"I sat there talking with a neighbor and then with Joe Wood until about eight o'clock. After he went away, I went over to the firehouse and there I seen the captain of the firehouse and Peter J. Bird. Then I went back again to the corner, the same place I was at before. I sat on the wall for a few minutes. Then I went over to the barbershop and I seen this barber, Louis Colossi, at the door. I was with him a few minutes. He was on the stand yesterday. I had been talking with him a few minutes and I asked him to lend me five cents and he said he could not spare it. That's all I remember him saying.

"I then went back to the wall. I stayed there until I saw Mrs. Buckley who asked me if I had seen the little girl that was missing, and I asked her what little girl it was. She told me, 'That Swedish girl that lives in the same house that I do.' I told her no I hadn't seen her. And she said, 'All right,' and went on.

"Johnny Dolan and Joe Woods came along, and they both sat on the wall with me until about ten o'clock, when one of them says, 'There must be a fire up in the flats,' and the three of us ran up together. We ran up to 1077 and 1075 Ogden Avenue, and I saw four or five people running across the street and I thought it might be a fire and they were running over to get the engines out. I got up there and found that they had found a little child in the cellar. I found that out in front of the house, I don't know who told me.

"There was a crowd gathering. We stood there for a few minutes and I seen Barney Valiunas standing in his doorway, and I went over and spoke to him for a while. We went inside and he gave me a drink I had no intention of paying for, and he knew that. I went in and got the drink and came out with him.

"Shortly after the ambulance left, I went upstairs and got into a long argument with my sister. I told her that if I didn't stop getting the devil off them, between her and my brother-in-law I would go away, and she said she didn't care whether I went away or not. I came downstairs disgusted, jumped right on a tram car and went right up and got to Mount Vernon, the city line, because the tram cars do not run any further, and I got out there to wait for a New Rochelle car where another sister of mine lived.

"I stayed with her until Conlan came up and asked me if I knew anything about the death of the little child in Highbridge and I told him I did not. He told me that the police were after me to get a statement, not to arrest me. They wanted to know if I had any suspicions on anybody. I told him I didn't have no suspicions about nobody. Conlan told me I had better come down because if the police got after me, they would lay the whole blame on me because I had gone away. I says, 'You are right,' and I came down with him.

"At the station house that night they brought me into a little room and took my fingerprints, and then Captain Morrison asked me if I knew anything and I told him no. He told me that if I had anything to do with this thing it would be better to tell him. I told him I didn't. I had nothing to do with the death of this child. He told me he was sure I was the right man, but he says, 'I don't think from your appearances or looks that you would do such a thing, but at the same time I think we have got you right.' I says, 'I don't know why.' He said, 'We have your fingerprints here and they correspond with the photograph of the child's neck,' he says. As he looked at them I kind of reached over and looked at them and he pulled back, he wouldn't let me see them. So then when he couldn't get me to say I had done it, which I didn't, he turns around and tells me what I could say."

*\*\**

I closed my laptop. The dream I had in Paris seemed to indicate I had fused and identified with a deeply repressed memory of being told about Ingrid Anderson, condensed further with reverberations of Anne Frank. But reading the Faulknerian prose of the transcript my sympathy also went out to the poor bastard MacBride. I'd gone to grade school in the Bronx with a big, lumbering kid named Johnny MacBride whose tie was always crooked, whose hands were always stained with ink, whose gray flannel trousers were thin at the knees. He received many paddlings from the creepy Irish Christian Brothers who pretended to educate us. I wondered if he was a descendant, perpetuating some genetic curse. The police captain, Captain Morrison, who overpowered MacBride, seemed the sort of man who would have been a friend of my family, a conniving, self-satisfied Irishman, an alpha mick up to no good, entirely at ease with rites of church and family. My father's older brother, Wild Jack, once worked as a property clerk for the Bronx police, the men who took "the bundle" for safekeeping. This story, that took place so long ago in a neighborhood I'd spent so much energy trying to forget, felt suddenly close. It gnawed at my psyche, unnerved me, shook me to the core.

# - Part Two -

*The Truth must dazzle gradually*
*Or every man be blind —*
                    —Emily Dickinson

## 17

Horcher was a relic. It had first opened in the 1940s thanks to a German chef who had cooked for Himmler in Berlin, but then moved to "neutral" Spain upon sensing the Third Reich was going to lose the war. Franco's Madrid was filled with Germanophiles back then, spies and scallywags of all stripes, and the restaurant had thrived ever since. It was decorated with deep red wallpaper set off by dark wooden trim and numerous displays of ceramic figurines. After Franco embraced Eisenhower in the 1950s, movie stars like Ava Gardner, Charlton Heston, David Niven, and Sophia Loren had flocked to the place with spouses, lovers, and retinues. Horcher remained a culinary stalwart even during the "Transition to Democracy," when the Spanish Socialist Party dominated the scene in the 1980s and '90s. Conservative Madrileños and left-leaning nouveaus were glad to walk through its doors, leaving large cars double-parked out front with the uniformed valet.

That night, more than two decades into the twenty-first century, it was three-quarters full with well-heeled parties still arriving. We were seated near a stained-glass window slightly opened to the avenue. As soon as she was seated, Carmen was provided with a footrest covered in burgundy velvet that had faded over time into a warm pinkish hue. It was deftly placed without fanfare. A small silver bucket filled with ice and radishes was brought to the table along with bread and butterballs. I ordered champagne. We toasted and took a sip.

"How did you know about this place, or did the hotel recommend it?" she said.

"No. I've been here before, a lunch with a bunch of people from the Prado some years ago. They filled me in on its colorful history. I remembered it as a place where you could actually have a conversation without having to yell."

"Unlike Casa Dani."

"Which I loved. Well, until we were interrupted."

"I know. That was unfortunate."

"So, who was that fellow, an ex of yours?"

"No."

"Really? He seemed besotted."

"Did you actually just use the word 'besotted'?"

"I did," I said, "and you're changing the subject."

"He … anyway, he's about something else entirely. But what if he had been?"

"I would have understood his feelings—completely."

"Have you been jilted by someone you care about?"

"Not since I was a teenager," I said. "Not really. Like you with your husband, I've generally been the leaver, not the left."

"But not always."

"Pretty much always. Well. Except for when I lost my mother. That was a double-whammy. Not only did she prefer my father to me, but then she left us both, which I expect goes a long way toward explaining why, since then, I've been the one to put a stop to things."

"So perhaps we're two of a kind in that regard," she said.

"Could be."

"On the verge perhaps of a battle royale."

On that we clinked glasses and drank some champagne.

"That's my sorry explanation, anyway," I said. "What's yours?"

"Wait a sec. Are you saying you leave the women you fall for because in the end you're afraid they'll eventually leave you like your mother?"

"I'm not proud of it," I said. "But I've done it enough times to make me stop and think. It's like I get to a point where I start to get anxious if things are going too well, and rather than work through it, rather than risk another catastrophe that would blow me out of the water, I—unconsciously, mind you—find an excuse to wreck things, usually by finding someone new."

"Now it's me who's worried," she said.

"Well, it's how life goes, no?" I said. "No matter how well things begin, they always end painfully, one way or the other, whether you're an eleven-year-old Ingrid Anderson, a six-year-old me who has to watch his mother die, or some theoretical happily married couple who eventually lose each other to illness and death."

"Wow," she said. "You are the *alegria de la fiesta.*"

"This place is a trip," I said, looking to change the subject.

"I completely agree," she said. "But you must be used to places like this."

"Not really. I tend to avoid them in Paris or London or New York. They intimidate me as a rule and serve heavy, too-elaborate dishes that give me indigestion. I prefer new places."

"New women. New restaurants. The pick of the litter."

"That's not fair," I said.

"I'm just kidding," she said. "I think."

That evening she wore a black dress and small gold earrings. Her blonde hair was down below her shoulders and on one finger she wore some sort of heirloom ring dotted with tiny old stones.

"So now that you've realized I'm a depressed, serial commitment-phobe, what about you?" I said.

"I'm not really one for armchair analysis," she said, "but I suppose, taking your cue, I behave in a somewhat similar fashion. My parents drifted apart and divorced when I was young. Not a dramatic thing these days but it was back then, here. He left the country and I lost touch with him for too long and I suppose I've been reluctant to trust men ever since. Let's just say I harbor a mix of low self-esteem and rage."

"I see."

"She remarried after a while, to a childhood sweetheart from Barcelona, but it was more of a rebound relationship. It didn't last very long and I didn't get along with him very well either."

"So, you've had a bit of a rough time."

"I really can't complain. I've been blessed as well."

We'd ordered fish and were just about done. I was tempted to renew the discussion about Ingrid Anderson and MacBride, but we were clearly in need of something cheerier.

"When do you go back to Boston?" I asked.

"Tomorrow."

"No."

"I told you," she said. "I only had a couple of days here."

"I know. I know. I suppose I didn't want to take it literally."

"What are your plans?"

"Back to Paris, to stay there until July to finish the Géricault article. My classes don't resume until the fall."

"You're so lucky to be on leave," she said. "What about July and August?"

"I'm not completely sure yet. How about you?"

"Apart from a conference or two I'm not sure yet either."

"Well, maybe we could see some of each other then."

"We haven't even finished our first dinner together," she said with a laugh.

"It's our second dinner."

"Alone I mean."

"You're stalling."

"Well, of course I'm stalling. I'll have to think about it."

"Please do," I said.

We shared some strudel with a scoop of vanilla ice cream, and both of us had a mint tea. I invited her back to the Ritz for a nightcap. She declined. She wanted to get back to her mother for a nighttime chat since her flight left early the following morning. The car was waiting outside and we both got into it.

"How do you feel about dogs?" I said.

"You mean as pets?"

"I saw one today and I've been thinking about getting one ever since."

"What kind?"

"A King Charles spaniel."

"What a grand name. Is it big or little?" she asked.

"Medium sized. Like twenty-five pounds, Yea high, yea long."

"I've never had a dog," she said, "or any kind of pet really."

"So, what do you think?"

"You should definitely try to get one if you want to."

"I mean, you don't hate dogs or are allergic to them?"

"Not at all," she said. "I think they're sweet. Though I don't like big dogs. They scare me. You might think of adopting one," she said. "There are loads of abandoned dogs in need of someone like you."

"Thing is, when you adopt, you never really know what you're getting."

I could sense this last comment of mine did not sit well with her. The car was already approaching the Parque del Oeste. I saw the Temple of Debod all lit up.

"We never got back to talking about the case," she said.

"Perhaps we will, soon."

"I'd like that," she said.

I walked her to the entrance of her mother's building, kissed her, and said goodnight.

## 18

I didn't read any more of the trial that night. I exchanged some text messages with Carmen, maintaining a line somewhere between flirtation and constraint. I was generally pleased with how things had gone, but frustrated. I'd wanted to find out more about the fellow who showed up at Casa Dani. Who was he really? How and when did they meet? What did this "about something else entirely" mean? The side of me commensurate with my age and experience told me to let it go, for it was none of my business, and she seemed relieved and grateful to me for not pressing harder. But a needy insecure side of me wanted to ask her about it.

I tried to put it out of my mind by phoning the concierge's desk to see if they could find me a breeder or a good quality pet store in the area that might have a King Charles spaniel puppy available. Twenty minutes later, close to 3 a.m., there was a discreet knock on my door followed by an envelope being slipped underneath it. On thick Ritz stationery, written with a fountain pen, was a list of breeders and stores with their respective phone numbers and websites. I felt ashamed for putting them through such trouble at such an hour. It seemed at once like the sort of service the Ritz might get off on providing, and a spoiled American's request. It was then that I remembered Carmen's suggestion I try to adopt a dog and how she had reacted to my lack of enthusiasm. So I googled pet adoption services in Madrid and in the surrounding area. I decided to go for ones outside the city, thinking they might have healthier options. I found one I liked the looks and sound of in a region called La Vera, about two hours west of Madrid.

I phoned the pet adoption place and left a message. Tired of being driven around, I had the hotel rent me a car the next morning, and after sending Carmen a bon voyage message I found my way onto the A5 highway out of Madrid heading toward Extremadura.

Around the time her plane took off, I had stopped for a coffee at a roadside café near a village called Santa Olalla.

It was dark inside, and I stood at the bar like a Spaniard. A TV was on, but nobody was watching. A selection of CDs with racy covers was on display just to my left. I enjoyed the noise of milk being steamed and the thudding sound the barman made knocking used coffee grounds into a wooden drawer under the espresso machine. I saw no women about, just local men who seemed comfortably unemployed.

The woman I'd met in Paris and followed to Madrid was jetting north by northwest somewhere above me that very moment, in an Iberia Airbus on its way toward Santiago de Compostela, from where it would veer west and initiate a transatlantic crossing. Seven hours later she'd see the coast of Newfoundland and then our mutually shared Commonwealth of Massachusetts.

I was glad to be out of the city. That part of Spain was beautiful at that time of the year. All the plains were green and blowing. Poppies sprouted everywhere, drawing the eye to deep red stains in the tall grasses of undulating fields. The Gredos mountain range rose in the distance. The air was clean, the light bright and fresh, the temperature mild, the coffee with hot milk served in a Pyrex glass with half a sugar cube delicious. Back in the car that smelled new, I felt autonomous and optimistic. It was pleasurable finding my way to the adoption fellow's village.

When I got there and drove through it there was little to recommend it apart from the gorgeous surrounding scenery. The man's "chalet" was just outside the village, a one-story brick structure that looked unfinished. I knocked on the door and a great barking surged from within, basso, alto, and soprano. Jose Antonio was tall and portly and very charming. He was an elementary school teacher who ran this service pro bono in his spare time. Many of the dogs ran around us as he told me how some of them had come to be there. The house smelled of animals and damp and was starkly appointed with haphazard furniture. He lived for the dogs.

I followed him into a small room in the back of the house where there was a round table and some simple chairs and on the floor a large, round plastic tub with some ruined cushions in it and three dogs younger than the ones that had greeted me. I saw the one I wanted immediately. It was black with a white chest and white front paws. It was the smallest of the three, but it looked at me intensely as the other two continued to fall over themselves while trying to rip apart a small cardboard box. Jose Antonio made us tea and told me about the little fellow. It was what he termed a typical story, a puppy that had been given to a child for Christmas only to be abandoned six months later, on the side of a highway, when it was time to go to their summer home or condo, by which point the novelty had worn off. I found it hard to believe, but he assured me it happened all the time. He had named the little dog Lobezno, which meant "little wolf." He thought it might be either a purebred or mix of a Tibetan terrier with something else. He assured me it had been checked out and given its requisite shots and dewormed and that the little guy would not grow to be much larger than thirty pounds. We did paperwork, I gave him a donation, and then he put the dog in a carrying case.

I drove to Jarandilla de la Vera to get some pet supplies and had a grilled ham and cheese sandwich and a Diet Coke for lunch at another bar. In no hurry to return to Madrid, I drove to the parador in the town of Oropesa where, according to a website, Frank Sinatra and Ava Gardner once stayed, in a special room called the Cardinal's Suite. I booked it en route. Oropesa was not an attractive town either, but the parador, some sort of castle from long ago, was beautifully refurbished and had a swimming pool hidden by tall hedges draped in honeysuckle. No pets were allowed, but I snuck my new companion in and gave the head maid a bit of cash to look the other way for a night.

The suite had a large bathroom and two sitting rooms and then a narrow hall that led into an elaborate, turret-shaped boudoir dominated by a vast, canopied bed with a painted headboard. I'd nabbed a bunch of newspapers from a table near the reception desk that I spread out on the floor for the puppy to play on. He was reluctant to come out of the carrying case when I set it down and opened it, but eventually he did, and we had our first serious chat. I told him who I was and what was in store for him and he listened with what I can only describe as nobility.

In the late afternoon I went down to the pool and being the only one there went for a quick swim in my boxer shorts. Back up in the room I played with the puppy, took a nap, woke up and thought about Carmen.

That she might already be crossing the Charles River into Cambridge was difficult to believe. Though I'd flown across the Atlantic countless times, it never did anything to dilute my sense of wonder. I sent her a photo of the puppy, underlining the fact that I had adopted it, and asked her to think of a name for him. I saw he'd done some of his business on the newspaper and I cleaned it up. He'd found one of my socks and was playing with it, rolling around like a kitten, making little growling noises. I ordered some dinner from room service.

In the suite that night I did all I could to not tell Carmen how much I wished that she were there with me. What I did tell her was that I'd all but made up my mind to return to New England sooner than later. As I prepared to go to sleep, I encouraged the puppy to get up on the bed with me. It was high and he was little still. But he didn't want to be picked up. It seemed I was dealing with the fallout of some past trauma. In the end I stripped the bed and arranged the sheets and the coverlet and the pillows on the hard floor and we fell asleep together like that.

I woke at dawn. The puppy was asleep at my feet. Two of the five windows arranged in a semicircle had their curtains drawn open, revealing an ochre-toned cathedral nearby bathed in soft pink light. There was a large nest in the bell tower with a stork sitting in it, preening itself. Swallows swooped and darted about the roofs and the whitewashed walls of houses closer by. I opened one of the windows so as to be able to listen to them and got back under the covers on the floor. The puppy woke up, looked at me, and went back to sleep. It was too early to order breakfast, and I was feeling lazy but too awake to close my eyes again.

It could not have been a less familiar place. A parador in the middle of nowhere at the edge of a town I knew nothing about, in a country where I hardly spoke the language. And yet I felt content and at ease. The anonymity and the isolation were a relief. The surroundings were unexpected and appealing. I wondered if Sinatra and Ava Gardner had really been there in that room back in the day, drinking and screwing and brushing their teeth together, the skinny tenor from Jersey and the gorgeous North Carolinian hick, the two of them feeling even more alienated than I did. I remembered that my father met Sinatra a few times, at Jilly's in New York, and that he had spent a boozy weekend with him in Palm Beach with JFK before the latter's inauguration.

Just as I was about to get up, I received an email.

*Shaun,*

*I thought about our conversation at Horcher's last night. BTW, I really am happy you went ahead and adopted your little dog who looks adorable.*

*I forgot to mention that my father was a painter. His mother was Italian, a teacher of mathematics, his father a textile manufacturer from St. Petersburg, Russia, who fled to Milan where he met his bride shortly before the Bolshevik revolution. Mother met my father in Rome where he was working as an apprentice for a classic portraitist. She was on a university trip. They fell in love. He left Italy because of her and came to live in Spain. Once there his mostly figurative work changed. He fell under the influence of a school of new Spanish painters, like Saura and Guerrero and Zóbel. You may not be familiar with them or this period. He got caught up in their world and often got into trouble with the Franco authorities. Though he wrote to me faithfully after the divorce, I never responded, first out of anger, then out of embarrassment. Driving down the Amalfi coast one night he and his second wife and their two children had a horrific accident. He was the sole survivor. Shortly before I married Matthew, when I was in Italy for a scientific congress, I went to see him. He was in terrible shape. He hugged me and would not let me go until we both collapsed in an ocean of tears and regret. I stayed with him for as long as I could. We wrote to each other often after that and discovered numerous similarities.*

*Then, in the midst of my awful marriage, I received word of his sudden death. When I left Boston on this latest trip, before I went to Spain, before I went to Paris and met you, I flew first to Milan and visited his grave where he is buried next to his parents. When Consuelo mentioned you to me, I think it was the fact that you are an art historian that most caught my attention. Anyway, I too have lived with sorrow and guilt. I don't know why it is so difficult for me to talk about this, but it is. I wanted you to know.*

*Xx Carmen*

I read it a few times as the light increased and the swallows continued their aerobatics outside. It made sense. Her hair and eyes and
cheekbones were sculpted from Russian genes, her coloring and
spirit were Italian and Iberian. People's lives. The illusion with which
we begin a romance, and then all the different ways it can go wrong
afterward. I pictured the accident along the Amalfi coast, shuddered,
and ordered breakfast. I read some more of the transcript. I was
almost finished with it.

- 19 -

**Eugene J. MacBride:** "Captain Morrison told me to say that I picked up the child and was fooling with her and let her fall accidentally and got scared away and all such a lot of stuff he was telling me. And how soon I could get out of it by telling this—how I couldn't get into any trouble—that they had to get somebody for it. He told me that he had to get somebody for it.

"I must have been in that room at the precinct house five or six times, in and out with different men, trying to get me to say that I had done this thing, them telling me it would be the best thing for me to do what Captain Morrison told me, that I would get out of this thing in twenty-four to forty-eight hours. I was getting pushed around from one to the other all night long.

"About three in the morning I was put in a cell. I stayed until about two o'clock the following afternoon. About every fifteen minutes someone would come in and wake me. I got sick of it. They kept on with it until around eight in the morning, not allowing me to lay down. I would like to know if I could get washed. Couldn't get no wash. Then I asked for a drink of water and some breakfast. I didn't get nothing until there was a couple of them coming in, running in and out three or four times, pounding me with a small stick that looked like one of them little billy clubs they carry. They didn't pound me with them, they just jammed them at me that way. I got it a couple of times here (indicating right breast). They didn't hit me in the face.

"Finally, they had me so I was crying. I didn't know what to do myself—came in there telling me 'You have to tell this.' I didn't want to tell it. I had no reason to tell it. I am not guilty of anything. It didn't make any difference. 'If you tell this thing you are not going to be held for it—maybe a couple of days and then you will get out of this thing,' they said, 'it is just that we want to get something to get this thing squashed. We ain't had no sleep either, we ain't had no more to eat than you did.' Have I got to suffer I says for somebody else who has committed this crime, for to let you people sleep? It didn't make no difference to them.

"I told them that if they would give me something to eat, I would tell them what Morrison told me. They brought me something to eat. It was while the door was open as they brought me something to eat that one of them had what looked like the butt of a gun and he held it to my head and says, 'Do you see that? Now look, don't forget what you said. Here is your meal.'

"The story I confessed to was not the truth. I did not at any time kill Ingrid Anderson. I did not take her up in my arms and while playing with her drop her down on the tiling of the vestibule of 1077 Ogden Avenue, or any other place. I did not see Ingrid Anderson on June 6, 1916, or on that day give her or any other child a penny. I don't know whether Captain Morrison ever saw me before Saturday night at the station house. He might have seen me before. I don't know. I never seen him. I have been a gardener. I have also been a foreman, taking charge of men. Also doing odd jobs around the neighborhood, doing anything outside of mechanical work. I started to earn my living when I was fifteen years of age.

"Captain Morrison is smarter than me and so I said what he told me to. I did not tell anyone that I had been forced into this statement because I was afraid. I have never had any trouble with Captain Morrison. I suppose the reason why he should want to send me to the electric chair on false evidence is to save himself. If they didn't get somebody for this thing, why, they would lose their sleep. That is all they were thinking about that Saturday night when they had me there. Nobody, at no point, ever said anything about the child being raped.

"I was living with the family of Conlans at 1077 Ogden Avenue. I did not have a separate room of my own there. I slept with Mr. Conlan himself. My brother-in-law. The Conlans occupy five rooms. They have three children. All the rooms are taken up by the family. I am not in the habit of playing with any girls or little boys. I associate with people of my own kind, my own age."

- 20 -

I closed the file and checked my email and found another from Carmen, who was clearly having trouble sleeping. She suggested I call the puppy Corru, after a small seaside town in Galicia named Corrubedo where there was a vast beach she loved. I thanked her for the story about her father and said I would love to see some of his paintings someday and that, yes, I would christen the puppy with the name she suggested and strive to roll those two r's together, but only on the condition she show me the town and beach at her earliest convenience. I found it on a map and was intrigued. I took a long shower and then took Corru out for his first walk.

I tried to make some sense of what I'd been reading. Were the coroner, the assistant DA, and all of the policemen lying for Captain Morrison, or was MacBride the liar, saying whatever he could to avoid being strapped into the electric chair? MacBride seemed too much of a simpleton to me, incapable of such guile and subterfuge. More than that, he did not come off as a rapist or a cold-blooded child killer, not that I had known any. And the timeline didn't hold up. Why wasn't that obvious? With so many people seeing him in so many places that day, afternoon, and evening, when would he really have had the time and opportunity to rape and strangle the girl in the basement and then return to the wall in such a calm manner? My gut told me that Captain Morrison—who I pictured as a kind of Hugh "Blazes" Boylan from Joyce's *Ulysses*—was the villain, and that he and his cops were thick as thieves, determined not to lose their case and look foolish. But of course I wasn't certain. I began to wonder why I cared so much.

Back in the room I phoned my travel agent in New York and, using little Corru as my excuse, had her book me a private plane back to Paris. Then I double-checked to see that his papers and health certificate were in order, packed, and put the little guy back in the carrying case. I paid for the room and drove directly to the Madrid airport. We landed at Orly around 6 p.m. and Thierry took me to the apartment. I fried myself an egg for dinner, ate it with toast and mar-malade, opened a cold Sancerre blanc, fed Corru crackers and little bits of ham and cheese, and then went back yet again to try to get to the end of the transcript. On behalf of "the People," police witnesses were called to knock down MacBride's testimony.

***

**Frederick A. Buddemeyer:** "I am a policeman. I went to the house of the defendant's father and brought him to the station where I left him sitting in a chair. Then he was taken into Captain Morrison's room. By the time I left the station house around 1:30 a.m. the prisoner had already been locked in the cell. I did not visit him there. I did not at any time strike him or threaten him or see anybody else do it. I treated him like a gentleman."

**Eugene Whalley:** "I am a policeman. On June eighth I was on the night shift at the station house. I was in charge of the cells and prisoners. I received the defendant from Officer Buddemeyer and locked him up around 2:00 a.m. I did not from that time admit anyone else into the cell corridor. I did not refuse the defendant a drink of water. I never did that to a human being in my life. I did not keep him up all night by asking him questions. I don't recall speaking with him at all that night."

**William Wilkesmann:** "I am a policeman. I relieved Officer Whalley at 8:00 a.m. that Sunday morning. During that morning I did not admit anybody to the cells to see MacBride. I served him his dinner that day. After he finished his meal, I took him out and presented him to Captain Morrison upstairs."

**John F. O'Mara:** "I am a policeman and first saw the defendant at the station house. I at no time told him that he should tell the story suggested by Captain Morrison. I never heard that Captain Morrison had suggested a story for him to tell."

**Theron R. Jameson:** "When I received the message that the defendant was ready to make a statement, I went to it right away. Captain Morrison was with me. I did not notice anything peculiar about the defendant's condition. He was dirty, his collar was dirty, and his hair not brushed. That is all I noticed. He did not make any statement to me about ill-treatment of any kind. After the examination was over, I went and got my lunch. I did not see the defendant again after I left that room."

Paris felt different. I sensed Carmen's presence everywhere, in the apartment and during the walks I took that either followed or intercepted the routes we'd taken together. Up until then I had not felt lonely there. Clearly, I was indeed besotted. Associating her with Dirk and Consuelo, I gave them a call and reached Dirk on his cell phone in Ireland, where he was scouting locations for his film. He told me Consuelo and Lucia were still in Paris and I got them over for tea and some pastries I picked up at the Boulangerie Martin.

It was a warm spring day and they arrived in sneakers and summer dresses, Consuelo very pretty in a sculptural way, somewhat resembling Françoise Gilot during her Picasso period. Lucia looked more like her father. Corru was a hit with both of them, but once we settled in the living room and poured tea Consuelo got down to business, which was just what I wanted.

"Are you in love with her yet?" she asked, half in jest.

"Yes," I said. "I am."

It caught her by surprise. She raised a hand to her chest.

"Really?"

"I've got all the symptoms."

"Does she know?"

"I'm afraid she might," I said. "I've been none too subtle about it."

"This is such good news," she said.

"It'll be good news if it's reciprocated. I think there may be another guy involved, or that there was not that long ago—or something. I met her in Madrid, and we ran into him, embarrassing everyone, but I finally got her out to dinner with me."

"Oh my god!"

"Don't tell me she hasn't told you all this."

"She hasn't. We're not that close, you know. Who was the guy? That must have been just amazingly awkward."

"It was. But she handled it very well. I've no idea who he is. But she says he's not someone to be concerned about."

"See? She's into you too."

"She's amused at least—I hope. She plays her cards close to her chest."

"*Claro*. Good for her."

Consuelo had an accent that was hard to place, part French and part Spanish, and some of it possibly invented, a Euro-aristo intonation contoured for effect.

"Tell me more about her," I said. "And don't tell her I'm head over heels. I've already come on way too strong, which is not sexy."

"I don't agree."

"You think?"

"Have you told her how you feel?"

"No. I'm not that insane. It's too soon."

"Well, so you're playing your cards close to your chest too."

"Anyway," I said, not wanting to go there. "She's delightful and I'm so grateful to you for thinking of me. It was the last thing I expected."

"I just had a feeling about you two."

"I hope you're right."

"I'm jealous," she said, standing and looking at herself in the large mirror over the fireplace. "I haven't felt like you're feeling for a long time. Enjoy it."

"I can't eat or sleep, but I am enjoying it."

Lucia was playing with Corru. No matter how many times her mother and I told her not to, she kept trying to give him one of the pastries. I finally had to take the platter away.

"I want a dog too, *maman*."

"Talk to your father about it," Consuelo said. "It's a lot of work."

"Is it?" I asked her.

"For most people it is."

"Tell me," I said. "How long *has* it been since you've felt this way?"

"Do you have anything stronger to drink?"

"Champagne?"

"That would be lovely."

It was too early for me. Gold light was still streaming across the river onto the living room carpets. When I returned from the kitchen both Lucia and Corru were asleep on the couch.

"Look at that," I said in a whisper.

"They're very cute together," she said.

"I'd happily get her a dog."

"Dirk would kill me."

I poured her some of the champagne, a 1998 Pol Roger, very cold.

"God, that's good," she said taking a sip.

"Churchill's favorite. He drank it like water."

She took a swig of it.

"So, you were saying," I said.

"The last time I really felt that way was during my first year with Dirk. We were both with other people when we met, and all the secret meetings in hotels, the hurried trysts in borrowed apartments, was thrilling."

"How long did that last?"

"It lasted until we became a couple, you know, officially, out in the open, when I realized that the passion high had much to do with our having had to lie and sneak around."

"But you got married."

"Ours was a good story, and we looked the part for each other, you know. And, well, here we are still. We get along and respect each other and we're devoted to Lucia."

"This is clear to see."

She emptied her glass. I poured her another.

"Marriage is tricky, Shaun."

"I know," I said. "Everyone knows."

"You have to be very giving, and most people aren't. Or you have to be very lucky."

I had loved my wife too. But as Carmen had sussed out, I hadn't been *in* love with her.

"There was another time too," she said. "I've never spoken about it."

"You don't have to now." I'd never seen her like this.

"It was with a woman."

"Really?"

"A young woman."

"I can relate to that."

"But I'm not a lesbian," she said. "I mean, I've always been into guys, except for her. I could be bisexual, but I'm still processing the whole relationship."

"How young was she?"

"In her twenties. I don't know what came over me. *Une amitié amoureuse.* It was so intense."

"Did Dirk know?"

"No. God no."

"So what happened?"

"Nothing. I just had to live with it. She moved away two years ago and that was that. But not a day goes by that I don't think about her, like the story Bernstein tells in *Citizen Kane*."

"To what do you ascribe it?"

"I've no idea. I only know that if I'd been able, if the world would've permitted it, I would have done anything to stay near to her."

"Who are you talking about, *maman*?" Lucia said, eyes still closed.

"No one, dear. An old friend."

The child kept her eyes closed and turned over, facing away from us. Consuelo and I looked at each other.

"Perhaps we should get back to Carmen," I said.

"Yes," she agreed, finishing her second glass and putting it down decisively. "She had a number of beaus when we were living in New York together, but I never got the feeling she ever really fell for any of them. She had a good time. She has a talent for that. It speaks well of her. But she never, from what I saw and from what she told me then, never went mad for anyone in the way you and I have been speaking about."

"And they fell for her."

"I should say so. Yes."

"How many are we talking about?"

"Keep your shirt on," she said. "Nothing crazy. A normal load."

"What about the husband?"

"Never met him."

I saw them out a little later. I almost invited them to dinner, but Consuelo looked tired and seemed to still be caught up in the melancholy of her recollections. I gave her a hug.

"Life and its tricks," I said speaking gently into her ear.

She kissed me on both cheeks. The second one, imbued perhaps with the relief that follows confession, was harder than the first.

I dined alone at the Rotisserie d'Argent and brought my laptop with me. MacBride's lawyers brought forth some character witnesses.

\*\*\*

**William C. Martin:** "I reside at 2771 Marion Avenue, Bronx. I have known the defendant intimately for twenty years. I am a civil engineer and graduate of Fordham University. We were young men at Fordham together. His reputation for being a peaceable man is very good. There is nobody that knows him could believe Gene MacBride possibly did such a crime. It is absolutely repugnant to his character."

**Thomas Porter:** "I reside at 955 Ogden Avenue, Bronx. I am a fireman from the station directly across the street from 1077 Ogden Avenue. I've known MacBride for three years and know other people that know him. I have never heard anything bad about the man's character. His reputation is good. I have seen him work. He was not all the time hanging around that neighborhood, sitting on the wall and going to Valiunas's. Once in a while he might. He was working pretty steadily. I never seen him do any plumbing, except to go around with Mr. Conlan, carrying his tools, which implied that the man was working."

**Dennis D. Buckley:** "I reside at 1049 Ogden Avenue and am a fireman at the station located at 1080 Ogden Avenue. Everybody in the neighborhood knows MacBride. He has worked in my house and he has worked for my wife. He did odd jobs for almost everybody around that neighborhood. His reputation for being a peaceful man is very good."

**Michael Healy:** "I reside at 1015 Nelson Avenue, Bronx. I am a fireman stationed at 1080 Ogden Avenue. I know MacBride. His reputation in the community is good."

**Philip M. Hamilton:** "I reside at 1034 Ogden Avenue, Bronx. I am an alderman for the City of New York. I know other people that know MacBride from around the neighborhood. To the best of my knowledge and belief, his reputation is that of a quiet, law-abiding citizen."

***

While processing all this I devoured half a roast chicken and drank a young, slightly chilled pinot noir. No potatoes and no dessert. Walking back to the apartment, I stared at the residences lined up along the south side of the Ile, including mine and Dirk's, admiring their modest height and elegant construction. I looked down at the river that I never tired of contemplating. The Harlem River was the river of my childhood, then came the East and Hudson Rivers, all three of them wider, wilder, and deeper than the Seine. But the Seine as it went through Paris was the most romantic, and sinister, especially at night. It was the farthest from the sea. The temperate air carried the scent of blossoms and old moistened cobblestones. A half-full dinner boat slid under the Pont de la Tournelle. It aimed a line of flood lamps against the house fronts, magnifying the shadows of the trees that lined the Quai d'Orléans and the Quai de Bethune. Close to my front door I passed a couple leaning against the parapet, nuzzling each other in what was surely a prelude to sex. I envied them.

That night I discovered the original notes I'd made in order to remember the dream. They were in the pocket of my robe. I looked them over and realized I'd all but forgotten about the man standing next to the girl at the beginning, the one who watched her as she leaned down and cut the wire wrapped about her ankles. I'd written "Ed Wynn" and underlined it. Ed Wynn, an actor I'd no associations with except for the role he played in *The Diary of Anne Frank*, a role I could barely recall. I thought to try to watch the film again, to stream it or order it for quick delivery, but the idea made me anxious, which was interesting all by itself, a film I'd only seen once in my life when I was fifteen.

Then the penny dropped.

One of the most interesting characteristics of dreams is how often they condense various meanings and people into one. Ed Wynn as the bickering, pessimistic Mr. Dussell in the film certainly meant something in the dream. He represented anxiety, judgment, doom and gloom, and he provided a direct link to my memory of the story of a young girl condemned to death, all of this the result of hearing the police siren before I fell asleep that night. But I realized then, staring at my notes, that the actor's name, in and of itself, provided me with another clue. Ed Wynn. Edwin.

I returned to the transcript and found the reference. Two of the children who testified referred to Ingrid's little brother as Edwin. I remembered how that confused me when I first read it because in their testimony the parents called him Adranaxa—a name no child would put up with and one that, I assumed, had been shortened and transformed into Edwin. And then I remembered the only Edwin I'd ever known, if you could even call it that, a man I had not thought about since my early teens.

# - 22 -

When my father married Caro Cuddihy-Woodward, she was much younger than he was, as young as Carmen was in relation to me, which gave me thought. Right after their honeymoon we moved from our Bronx apartment on Undercliff Avenue into her duplex on Fifth Avenue. My father ceased renting houses each summer with the Judge and we began to summer at Caro's "cottage" at the beach in the Cuddihy-Woodward compound in Southampton/Water Mill. When they first started dating, she had a smaller house on the property, but by the time they married her mother had died, and her older sisters, content with their own homes, had allowed her to buy them out of their shares of the main house.

Initially designed by Stanford White, it faced the dunes and had a swimming pool. There were ten bedrooms on the second floor, each with their own bath, some with balconies overlooking the ocean. The third floor was a warren of smaller bedrooms reserved for servants. The main floor had a huge kitchen, dining room, living room, and study. About sixty yards away, backed up against a line of tall hedges, was a large garage that matched the house. It had its own repair shop, space for five automobiles, and an apartment upstairs where Edwin lived.

Caro was still alive at ninety-four. A decade after my father died, she sold the New York apartment and moved out to the house by the dunes permanently. In addition to her normal staff, two nurses took turns taking care of her. I spent most Thanksgivings and Christmases there and visited whenever I could. I called her that night before going to sleep.

"Da-ling," she said. She actually spoke like that, a family-specific version of debutante lockjaw *a la irlandés,* tweaked with a dash of Katharine Hepburn. She was angular and trim and slightly masculine the way the actress had been as well—a sportswoman, mostly tennis and swimming and a decent game of golf that she had worked at to please her father. Her mother, Mrs. Cuddihy, whom the Judge had courted in a nineteenth-century manner during their mutual widowhood, had been religious, retiring, and very smart. Rose Kennedy came to her often for advice. Caro was the youngest of the five daughters and the rebel among her sisters.

"Where are you?" she asked.

"Paris."

"Still?"

"Still, but not for long."

"Are you driving all the *jeune filles* mad?"

"Every single one," I said, smiling at the ceiling.

"Then pick a favorite, but not the prettiest, and marry her, for god's sake. Bachelorhood doesn't become you."

"I'm working on it," I said.

This was a theme she visited regularly, starting not more than a month after Scarlett died.

"Why not the prettiest?" I couldn't resist.

"She'll make you unhappy. It'll be all about her." It sounded like the voice of experience.

"How are you doing?" I asked.

"I'm well, marvelous. I've got a beau."

"Who is the lucky man?"

"The new gardener. He's Venezuelan. He brings me flowers."

"A Latin lover."

"Sí!"

I remembered the one and only time she came to our apartment in the Bronx. She inspected my father's closets and found half of them still filled with clothing that had belonged to my mother, stuff he'd been unable to throw out. She told him she would handle it and donate everything to a Catholic charity. He didn't resist. He seemed relieved. She'd seen us there, surveyed the shipwreck, and come to the rescue.

"I need a favor," I said.

"Whatever you wish."

"Do you remember Edwin the mechanic? From when I was a boy?"

"Yes. Yes, I do. Why? What about him?"

"Can you remember how it was he came to work for us?"

"I suppose I should, but I don't. Why?"

"I had a dream. And I was just wondering."

"About him? Are you going gay on me, Shaun?"

"No. Nothing like that."

"I wouldn't mind, you know."

"I've met a woman, one I truly fancy."

"Then introduce me to her before I run off with Javier." She pronounced it incorrectly, as Ja-Vi-Ay.

"I will. Her name is Carmen. She's Spanish."

"I always said you and I were the bohemians of the family."

Her voice sounded weaker than usual.

"How are you doing dear—really."

"Fit as a fiddle," she said, "more or less. A bit of heart trouble now and then."

I sent Carmen an email after I turned the light off and told her about this exchange. She answered straight away and said I hadn't mentioned that Caro was still alive. I apologized and told her I'd be in Boston in a few days. All she said was "How nice." I've always hated that word. But she did sound enthusiastic about having dinner with me when I got there.

The phone rang at three in the morning, waking me and making my heart race. I hoped it was Carmen, tipsy perhaps and more forthcoming. But it was Caro, who apparently paid no attention to the difference in time between Wickapogue Road and the Quai de Bethune.

"I remember now," she said.

I pictured her in her armchair, or perhaps in bed in the room she had shared with my father, at the far western end of the second floor. The two beds pushed together with separate Pratesi sheets and pillowcases. The three large Persian rugs handed down from the original Cuddihy residences in Albany and Brooklyn. The bureaus and the mirrored vanity table. Stacks of yellowing issues of *Vogue* and *Time* and *National Geographic*. The too-modern sliding door to the balcony she had installed. The scents of medicines and mildew, naphthalene and Chanel No. 5. I decided I should go and see her as soon as I could.

"Your father helped him," she said. "I remember him saying Edwin was someone he knew as a boy, that he'd been through a hard time. He spoke to the Judge who spoke to my mother and she hired him. She said the fellow's mother had worked for us straight off the boat from Sweden before I was born. Your father promised he would be reliable. And he was. Our cars never ran better."

It was Adranaxa. Ingrid's little brother. It had to be.

"Whatever became of him?" I asked, my eyes now wide open in the dark. "I don't remember when he left."

"He left all of a sudden. His mother took ill and he brought her back where she came from. I liked him, very much. We gave him a good severance check. He was a lonely fellow."

"How so?"

"Never had anyone with him, openly or on the sly as far as I could tell."

The summer after my mother was buried, I would walk about the property we rented at Fair Lea in Southampton, imagining adventures. I would stroll up and down the long driveway, run about the vast lawn, and play inside the forestlike thicket of untended hedges behind the house that separated us from the McKnight and McGowan estates. Throughout the day I would fixate on certain objects. I would look at twigs, stones, or stray bits of paper on the ground and grace them with sentiment. I could not bear the thought of their remaining abandoned and uncared for with the fall of night. And so I would pick them up and put them in my pockets.

At the end of the day I'd put all that I had rescued in the top drawer of a bureau in the room I shared with my father, which faced the ocean. At one point my Aunt Jane noticed the drawer filled with sand, pennies, pieces of wood, and paper. When she asked me, I told her the how and why of it. A devoted Catholic, unmarried, an attractive forty-year-old virgin who only pretended to have a beau now and then, a woman who lived with her father and who had a number of potentially crippling neuroses of her own, a woman with no patience for anything resembling modern psychology, she nevertheless understood what I told her, because she did not tell me to stop it. She simply listened and nodded as if my compulsion were the most logical thing in the world.

I grew out of it. More accurately, over time, it transmogrified and expressed itself in other ways that are still part of me. I'm all right saying goodbye to people, I can shake their hands, kiss them, look them in the eye and depart. But I'm not good at leaving places. When I was leaving the Ritz in Madrid, I took a final look out the window at the Prado. In the bathroom I took note of the still damp shower and tub, the sink with its small bottles of half-used products, the towels and floor mats. I looked at the bed, touched it, and quite consciously took in the sitting room for a final time before letting myself out. At the parador in Oropesa I repeated the exercise. There I included the newspapers in my ritual, still spread out on the floor in the baroque bedroom. I imagined the people who'd written the articles in them, the presses that ran them, the small trucks and drivers that delivered them to the villages in the area. Even when I dropped off the car at the airport in Madrid, I bid adieu to it with some emotion.

So, when it was time to leave my apartment in Paris, the procedure was more complicated. I'd been there for five months. Though I had entertained friends and a few ladies, most of the time I'd been alone and content, pleased with my routines and caprices, never bored or itching for change. I'd gotten good work done. I'd derived pleasure at almost every hour of the day looking out the tall open Baudelairean window-doors down at the Seine, across to the Tour d'Argent, gazing west at what was left of Notre Dame and at the Eiffel Tower in the distance.

Before I left, I said goodbye to every inch of it, including the washer and dryer, the two guest rooms that had never been used, the kitchen, my zinc and copper tub, the armoires, even the utility closet. Mad as it sounds, I left the building with tears in my eyes. Sitting in the back of the car with Corru, chatting with Thierry on

117

the way to the airport, I remembered the exterior of the building where Carmen's mother lived back in Madrid, and I pictured it still there at that moment. I pictured the ocean I was about to fly across, the reality of it, the terrain underneath it, the hotel room in Boston where I would spend the night. I pictured the house at Fair Lea— bought and tarted up, some years after our departure, by Gloria Vanderbilt—I pictured it as it used to be. I pictured Caro, at that moment hopefully asleep in her bed with the night beach in front of her. I revisited the Undercliff, Ogden, and Woodycrest Avenues from my past, and tried to picture them as they might be then at four in the morning, most of the storefront signage in Latino Spanish. I pictured my wife's and my father's graves in Southampton, my mother's in the Judge's family plot at Gate of Heaven cemetery in Valhalla, New York. And I pictured Ingrid Anderson's grave in Queens, her coffin under the earth, her remains, her bones and skull, the thick stitches from the autopsies long decayed, her burial gown dark and tattered, just as real and existent as my still living hands holding my little living dog.

# - 24 -

I had booked a room I liked at the modest and discreet Eliot Hotel in Boston. Though too close to Newbury Street's boutiques with its crowds of shoppers, it conserved authentic Back Bay elegance and it was just across the river from MIT. I hadn't told Carmen exactly when I'd be arriving. When I got there I checked in and took Corru for a walk in the narrow bit of park that runs along the Charles River.

The Parisian streets, with their trim, beautifully dressed men and women perched on traditional English bicycles, were replaced by earnest, mostly thick-set joggers with a Kmart fashion sense and cyclers arrayed in bright spandex, pedaling fender-free bikes designed to punish calves and thighs. But the river shimmered in late spring light and little sailboats dappled the water and there was the MIT campus on the other side, where the woman I was pursuing lived and plied her trade. Many people who saw Corru stopped and asked about him with a disarming American friendliness that put my faux Euro snobbery to shame. I found a bench near the water and sent Carmen a text. The thought of calling her made me too nervous.

*Man & dog gaze longingly at MIT.*
She answered a few minutes later.
*Just finished class. WHERE are you?*
*Back Bay near the Harvard Bridge.*
*Are we still on for dinner?*

*Harvest. 7 P.M.*
*Great.*

The "great" was much appreciated. Back in my room I fell into a deep sleep thanks to which I arrived fifteen minutes late at the restaurant. She was halfway through a vodka martini chatting with the barman.

"*There* you are," she said, kissing me on both cheeks. She smelled like real roses mixed with lemon rind. We had oysters and salad and lamb chops with a white wine that she preferred, and we laughed a lot. We mostly talked about movies, celebrities, literature, and other Boston restaurants we liked. We barely touched on biology, art history, or MacBride.

"Come back with me and meet the puppy," I said, as casually as I could.

"I'd love to," she answered, seemingly sincere, "but I have a class at nine in the morning."

"When do they set you free for summer?" I asked, quickly moving on.

"Eleven days from now," she said. "I can't wait."

"Have your plans firmed up at all?"

"Nothing written in stone," she said. "I'm supposed to give two talks in London in July, but I may cancel, I love canceling, and I should see my mother a bit more. Other than that, I'm not sure yet. You?"

We were lingering over the end of the meal, me with a glass of red wine I ordered instead of dessert, she with a cup of mint tea.

"Normally I visit Caro in Southampton for a couple of weeks and then I go back to Europe. The west of Ireland, London, back to Paris, I keep saying I'm going to rent a little place on the Cote d'Azur, the sort of place I doubt even exists anymore, but I've yet to do it."

"No plans to visit Highbridge, I see."

"No. I couldn't."

"Why?"

"The idea terrifies me, and I cannot tell you why. Some deep-seated, visceral rejection. I just keep it well-preserved in my own way in my head. The idea of actually seeing those houses and apartment buildings, those streets and parks again, seeing they're still there, or not, fills me with dread. I thought about this last week while I waited in the car in front of your mother's building, admiring how you were able to return to a place you'd grown up in, while I am unable to."

"But you do return to Southampton."

"That's different. I've had continuity with that part of the world since I was born and most of my associations with it are good ones."

"What about your house in Williamstown?"

"My house."

"You mentioned a house there, even though you live in Lenox."

"I have a house there, yes."

"A nice house?"

"Very nice. It used to belong to Cole Porter."

"Well, so why Lenox then?"

"The place is too big for me, for one thing. It's a nice house with lovely grounds and a pool and the whole deal, but I like having a bit of distance from where I work. I live in a hotel, just outside of Lenox."

"A hotel."

"A really nice one, quite deluxe, out of the way, a massive old mansion with acres of lawns and great food, European service. Great wine cellar."

She finished what was left of her tea.

"You're quite eccentric. Do you know that?"

"I think I'm just lazy. I like being comfortable and not having to deal with domestic things, help and all of that, and if I fancy taking someone to dinner, I prefer not to have a colleague seated at the next table. You don't have that problem here because you live in a city."

"A small city. This wouldn't have something to do with your wife, would it?"

"How so?"

"Well, you've the apartment in New York you maintain but don't use, where you also stay in a hotel instead. And now it turns out you do the same thing where you actually live and work most of the year."

"The apartment belonged to her husband's family and I still think of it as pertaining to them. She and I bought the place in Williamstown together."

"They're still two places you lived with her."

"I see your point. And perhaps to confirm your theory, we didn't buy the Cole Porter house until she first got sick. We'd gotten to like the area over the years because Scarlett loved classical music and we'd often get to Tanglewood. Rather than sit out her chemo sessions in the city, we decided to move north. The job at the Clark opened up and soon after, the teaching position at Williams that's associated with the Clark, and so we bought the place there."

Added to the wine and the jetlag was the worry she might think I was carrying more baggage than she had counted on.

"Maybe you should sell them," she said. "The apartment in New York, and the place in Williamstown. Start fresh."

"I have thought of it. That's where the lazy part kicks in."

"Have you come here ahead of schedule because of me?"

The question came out of nowhere and though I felt off balance enough as it was, I just went for it. "Yes."

"So you're not lazy about that."

"No. Look. Could you come and visit this weekend? I'll fly you there. I can get a car to take you from MIT to Hanscom Field, a little airport not far from here, and a plane to get you to Pittsfield, forty-five minutes door to door. You can see everything and see what you think, and we can spend some time together. I'll get you a room at my hotel, it's called the Wheatleigh, look it up. You'll get a kick out of it."

She thought about it and to my great relief she then agreed. I walked her back to her place, a floor-through in Cambridge that was midway between Harvard and MIT. We kissed at the bottom of stairs that went up to a front porch. Really kissed this time. I flagged a cab and went back to the Eliot and took Corru out, up the middle of Commonwealth Avenue for a few blocks, then came back and went to sleep.

## 25

M r. Northshire was the district attorney, the job my father later filled, and Tannenbaum was one of MacBride's lawyers.

*** 

**Mr. Northshire:** "The People rest."

**Mr. Tannenbaum:** "The Defendant rests. I move for the dismissal of the indictment on the ground that the People have failed to show facts sufficient to constitute a crime."

**The Court:** "Motion denied."

**Mr. Tannenbaum:** "I also move to strike out all evidence with relation to the clothing worn by the deceased and removed and subsequently marked in evidence, on the ground that no connection is shown between the clothing and this defendant."

**The Court:** "Motion denied."

**Mr. Tannenbaum:** "I also move to strike out all testimony with reference to the alleged confession, on the ground that the same was not obtained according to law."

**The Court:** "Motion denied. The defendant is indicted for one of the highest crimes known to the law, murder in the first degree. It is charged that the defendant, Eugene J. MacBride, on the sixth day of June 1916, in the Borough of the Bronx, County of New York, from a deliberate and premeditated design to effect the death of Ingrid Anderson, did with malice aforethought, choke, suffocate, and strangle the said Ingrid Anderson, of which choking, suffocating and strangulation the child did then and there die. The People further claim that the defendant engaged in committing the crime of murder either before or pursuant to committing the crime of rape in the first degree upon Ingrid Anderson."

## 26

I got to the Wheatleigh around lunchtime. My suite was held on a yearly basis, so all my things were as I'd left them; some paintings I favored, shelves of books I treasured, two closets and a big bureau filled with mostly winter clothing. The grounds and gardens were in full bloom. The pool was filled and open. The staff was pleased to have me back. Corru presented the only wrinkle but I managed to iron it out with a donation.

My 1974 Citroën SM was in their garage. It fired up just fine and I drove it into town for a late lunch at the local café. The usual crowd was there, rich yoga ladies, graying trust-fund guys with iPads trying to look busy, some younger folk, including two gamins in tight jodhpurs who looked as if they might actually have been riding earlier in the day.

Back at the hotel I parked in the lot that bordered on a small forest, stepped back, and admired my car. When did automobiles start to get so ugly? I realized I was glad to be back, glad to be able to stop traveling for a time. After the extended calm of my Parisian stay, the past two weeks had been frenetic. Other wealthy people I knew were on the move constantly. It was like their job. Too anxious to stay in any one place for more than a week, they seemed to be slaves to invented calendars. I never wanted that to happen and I reassured myself with the thought that all my recent locomotion had been due to an exceptional circumstance. Carmen was a worthy cause.

It was a warm afternoon and I took Corru with me down to the pool, where I fell asleep under an umbrella. As was often the case there, no one else was around. When I woke up, I swam laps for a while. Corru ran about the edge until I got out and cuddled him. Back in my room I worked on the Géricault article and then breezed around the Internet looking into what had become of some of the people who had figured prominently in the MacBride trial.

Theron Jameson, the assistant DA who took MacBride's official statement at the police station, went on to be elected to Congress. Albert Vitale, one of MacBride's lawyers, became a judge and a key Tammany Hall Democrat leader in the Bronx, whose reputation was later ruined due to ties with underworld gangsters. Captain Samuel E. Morrison, the man I was most interested in learning about, went missing a few years after the appeal trial concluded. In a brief obituary that appeared once he was declared officially dead, one I found in the archive of the *New York Times*, two things caught my attention. Morrison had been trained, mentored, and brought along on the coattails of New York City Police Inspector Thomas F. Byrnes, a Dublin-born, firefighting, mustachioed figure straight from Scorsese's *Gangs of New York*. Byrnes was famous for his brutal physical and psychological interrogations of suspects. Though the MacBride case did not merit mention in Morrison's obit, another case he "solved" was cited, the rape and murder of another blonde twelve-year-old girl, found in the basement of a building less than a mile from Ogden Avenue.

I searched for this case and learned the crime had taken place in July 1916, one month after Ingrid's death. The similarities were striking. The suspected murderer was found dead from an apparent suicide, a gas tube from a stove stuck in his mouth, in a seedy one-room flat on the Lower East Side. The young man left a note that ended with the following words: "I'm sorry I done it, but I got crazy, as I often do, and you can't blame me or anyone. It was caused by the beautiful make up of women." I searched for more cases and found yet another. In June 1914, two years before Ingrid's murder, an eight-year-old girl named Veronica Brennan was strangled to death in the cellar of a tenement house on Second Avenue and 117th Street. She was left by the coal bins. The marks on her neck were identical to Ingrid's. Two "Italians" had been sought for this crime. They were never found.

Might the same person have committed all three murders? Captain Morrison was involved in two of the investigations. Though I searched extensively, I found no evidence of anyone who'd thought to link them together. Or was it just that young girls in big cities are always at risk from damaged men?

Alexander J. Conlan, the plumber married to MacBride's sister, in whose apartment MacBride was living on the night of the crime, had split up with his wife by the time of the appeal trial. He died five years later in a flu epidemic. The Andersons had also left the neighborhood by the time of the appeal trial, moving across the Harlem River into Manhattan. There was something about them. The disembodied tones of their testimonies stuck with me. I had the feeling they were hiding something. A sordid Nordic noir side of me even contemplated the possibility that perhaps they'd been involved in some way. Which led me again to the quiet, barely mentioned Edwin—Adranaxa Anderson—with whom, it seemed, I had a direct link thanks to my father, the Judge, and the Cuddihy-Woodward clan. Might the solitary life that Caro had described to me over the phone—assuming it was true—have been due to something surrounding the trauma of his sister's death?

The Pittsfield airport is two miles from the center of town, a town that was once a thriving city with factories, a museum, and an opera house. In 1851 it was the closest outpost of civilization to Herman Melville's Arrowhead estate where, far from the sea, he wrote *Moby-Dick*. The end of the twentieth century and beginning of the twenty-first had not been kind to any of the mill towns in northwestern Massachusetts. Plants closed, real estate values dropped, education flagged, and places like Pittsfield took on a sorry pallor. Starting in 2015 or so, things began to improve, and the place was picking itself up, opening some decent restaurants and a new hotel, but in general I tended to avoid it.

As soon as Carmen stepped off the little jet, I drove us straight back to Lenox. We went along Church Street and then took Route 183 west, out past the Tanglewood Music Center before turning onto Hawthorne Road, named from the time when Nathaniel Hawthorne lived on it, renting a little red house with his wife and young children that had since been destroyed and replaced with a facsimile. It looked down at rolling fields interrupted by patches of pine forest, ending at the spacious Stockbridge Bowl, where the author was said to have swum every morning.

I was nervous, of course, wanting everything to look and be just right. Carmen loved the puppy. She dug the car. She had a vague memory of Lenox. And as I hoped, she was bowled over by the

Wheatleigh as we glided in through its reclusive, winding, land-scaped driveway. I pointed out that it was originally built in 1893 as a wedding gift from a wealthy father to his daughter to celebrate her marriage to a penniless Spanish count. They were glad for the Spaniard's title and hired Frederick Law Olmsted to do the grounds. The couple summered there in robber-baron luxury for the rest of their lives.

Carmen's room was next to mine with its own monster bed, massive fireplace, and massive old-fashioned bathroom that was equipped with a plethora of high-end beauty products. She shared the same view as mine as well, out through tall, beautifully crafted windows of thick old glass, looking at the gardens that led down to the pool.

"I thought we might relax and hang out here for what's left of the day and night and then see the house in Williamstown tomorrow."

"Sounds perfect," she said.

She wore white jeans, a black blouse, a short, light denim jacket, and a slightly raised pair of velvety navy sneakers. It was around three and we took Corru to the pool, where to my dismay another couple occupied two of the chaise longue beds at the far end. Both of them exuded an air of complacency. The woman's flowery green, stiff, one-piece bathing suit might have come from Talbot's or from Lord & Taylor before it closed. She wore a wide-brimmed straw hat spiced up with a bandana, and oversized sunglasses through which she was reading a novel by Ann Patchett. The gentleman was balding and wore wire-rimmed glasses and was engrossed in the latest Stephen King. He was wrapped in his own yellow terrycloth robe that bore some kind of oversized club insignia on the breast pocket. A pair of brown, well-worn, well-polished tasseled loafers lay on the grass next to him.

I grabbed us some extra towels from a stack at the bottom of the garden stairs and guided us to the opposite end. Carmen dragged her chaise onto the grass and into the sun while I let mine stay where it was in the shade of a large umbrella. Corru went sniffing around the borders of blossoming shrubs. A distinct whine from maintenance men cutting the grass on the great lawn nearby was also a source of minor irritation. But Carmen seemed happy and proclaimed the entire setting divine and that the prospect of doing nothing but lying by the pool was her idea of heaven and that she'd worried I might be one of those anxious Americans tied to the dreary plow of illusory self-improvement in need of constant activity and distraction.

"Quite the contrary," I said. "Like I told you the other night. I'm lazy and like nothing better than just lying around."

"The plane was amazing, by the way," she said. "I've been pretending to be blasé, like it's the kind of thing I'm used to, which obviously I'm not."

"I hope it wasn't too rocky."

"Not at all. And the pilots, the super attractive gay steward, the whole thing was out of a movie. I don't want to think about what it cost. Half a year's salary for all I know. If I told anyone at work how I got here I'd lose tenure."

"Mum's the word."

This conversation was mostly fueled by mutual nerves regarding the reveal about to take place. She delivered what was for me a coup de grace, overpowering my Irish heart, when she stepped out of her sandals and took off the hotel robe to lie down and apply some sunscreen. She was wearing a small black bikini and looked amazing. Though neither of us would admit it, we were surely aware of the moment as being a first between us, seeing each other so nearly naked in sunny daylight. I noticed the gentleman at the other end of the pool interrupting his reading to steal a glance over the top of his glasses.

131

Then it was my turn. When I was younger, I was a fine specimen, lean and fit without being overly muscled and with no strange growths of hair in aesthetically challenging places. But I have never exercised, at least in the programmed way everyone seems so obsessed with, and I liked my food and wine. I wasn't fat by any means and my legs were still long and strong, but I'd gone somewhat predictably soft around the middle. Anyway, I got it over with when she wasn't looking and just lay down. She took me in without making it obvious and we went on talking as if it were the kind of thing we'd done for years.

In less than an hour, as shade from some tall trees began to drift across the pool area, the other couple gathered their things and left. They'd hardly spoken a word to each other. We went for a swim and Corru started barking until I got out. Emerging from the chilly water and drying off on a towel spread on the grass while Carmen swam laps, I stared at the sky and closed my eyes seeing red through my eyelids while listening to her steady strokes.

She got out and put her towel down next to mine.

"Feels great, doesn't it?" I said after a while.

That neither of us had felt a need to say something right away pleased me.

"God yes," she replied.

The kind of god I imagined her calling forth in that two-word response was one I could relate to, a Dionysus or a Pan. I wanted to kiss her. After a final swim we walked back toward our rooms. The lawns and gardens, the surrounding forest and the small flowering trees that lined the graveled path, the statues stained with dried moss—all of it was blessed by the sun's diminishing glow. Everything was tinted in peach and orange tones. It would have been the perfect time to take her by the hand and lead her into my room. But it was still too soon, or I was still too shy. Instead we retired to our respective rooms, our respective laptops and cell phones, and to our own beds for a lie-down.

I lay there and pictured her in the room next door, wondering what she was thinking, what she might be communicating to some girlfriend or confidante. Though un-annunciated the chemistry was there, plain to the both of us. It had been plain even on that first night in Paris at Dirk and Consuelo's. I went back there in my mind, to my bedroom on the Quai de Bethune that would be in the dark at that hour, my clothes in the closets and drawers, the antique walking sticks in the large Chinese vase by the front door, the river outside.

Before dining there at the hotel, we met as if for a date out on the slate-covered patio. We sat in chairs with a view of the vast sloping lawn that rolled down to the forest. We were offered champagne, but she chose a vodka on the rocks and I a Sancerre blanc that came from my own stash I kept there, something I didn't mention. The sun had set but true twilight had yet to settle in. She was radiant and looked rested and had some color. She wore a navy silk jumpsuit and black heels and her hair was down.

The only other people near us sat at a round table, a group of well-heeled Brits of a certain age and class who might have stepped out from an issue of *Country Life* or *Hounds*. The men had ruddy cheeks and puffy thick fingers, including pinkies strangled by battered signet rings turned just so. All of them drank champagne, the expensive stuff, and I assumed they were there for the music festival that was getting underway that week.

"It is so beautiful here," Carmen said as we clinked glasses. "I totally understand why you live here."

"Thank you for saying that."

"No. I really do."

It *was* beautiful, and private. I'd no idea how the place managed to stay afloat with such high rates and so few guests. But that evening, sitting with her, it also felt a tad stodgy, and though I was pleased to see her so content, I experienced an undercurrent of embarrassment, already envisioning that were we to get together and manage to live together some day, she would tire of this and come to view it as some kind of high-end retirement home. On the other hand, there was little chance of that happening any day soon. We worked at institutions located almost four hours away from each other.

"I often worry this place will go out of business when I least expect it," I said.

"Well, you always have your actual house as a fallback plan."

I smiled and nodded at her ironic tone. "Yes, I do."

Over dinner we talked about Edwin Anderson.

"You don't remember him? Come on. This is key," she said, those hazel eyes opening wide.

"He was the car guy, the garage guy, a guy who kept to himself. I only remember a slim fellow with a hawkish face who wore a kind of khaki uniform with an oily rag sticking out of his back pocket. I was a teenager with other things on my mind."

"Don't tell me you weren't into cars," she said. "Look at the one you're driving."

"Well, that's true." She had a point.

"I do remember him as a benign presence," I said, making an effort to recall him. "He had a certain nobility about him, and his reticence was intriguing."

"Jesus, he was Ingrid's brother," she said. "I can't believe it. Your dream begins to take on all kinds of new intimations."

"Another sort of weird thing is that, after I ran away from home for a few months when I was sixteen—I just refused to stand another year of Jesuits—I worked out a deal with my father and Caro and ended up spending my senior year living above the garage in

Southampton—I graduated from the local public school there. I lived in the same apartment where Edwin had been so many years."

"I don't get how you turned out the way you did," she said.

"How so?"

"Your father was a district attorney, and then some kind of killer lawyer. Didn't he want you to follow suit?"

"He did. But I didn't. And after I ran away from home, I pretty much negotiated my own ticket."

"A rebel."

"A rebel with patent leather dancing pumps."

She laughed. I continued.

"I think my life would have been very different had my mother not gotten ill and died. Even with my interest in art and the humanities, it would have been difficult to rebel with her around. I might have been coerced into law school. My father wouldn't have married Caro—with all that led to in my life. There's a fair chance I would have married someone more conventional."

\*\*\*

Deep into the night a gentle knocking on my door awakened me. I got out of bed, put my robe on, and kept the lights off. She came right into my arms, burying her face against my shoulder. I pulled her in and closed the door. She took off her robe, and in the darkness, I watched her climb into my bed and get under the covers in panties and a T-shirt. I joined her and held her for a while. We were sleepy and excited at the same time. Corru hardly stirred. Wise enough to let nature take its course, we hardly said anything. It was as if all of our banter up until then, our nervous commentary and conversation, fell away like scaffolding, like the cracked shell of an egg, broken by the force of an instinct unwilling to remain hidden any longer.

I woke again at five. Silence pervaded the room. A linen sheet and a cashmere blanket covered us. The hotel gardens and Berkshire forest surrounded us. I watched her sleep.

My life began playing stoopball in the Bronx and riding waves in the Atlantic Ocean. I'd lost my mother. I'd traveled the world and known pleasure and pain. I'd had a marriage of sorts. I dedicated energy to educating young people about the value of art in this unforgiving universe. Carmen studied the matter we're made of. There were things stored in her brain sleeping next to me, of towering sophistication, stored as yet more folded proteins, cheek by jowl with memories of smells and places, lights and caresses, all of them, like mine, en route to extinction, to be reduced someday to roadkill.

At dawn the smallest bit of light crept through a gap in the thick curtains. I smelled her hair. She stirred and rolled into me. Our hands began to wander. It was good to be alive.

# - Part Three -

*How can'st thou endure without being mad?*
—Herman Melville

# - 28 -

**The Court:** "The People have presented for your consideration two classes of evidence. The first class refers to circumstantial evidence and relates to the acts and conduct of the defendant on the day the body of the deceased was found in the cellar of the house at 1077 Ogden Avenue in the Borough of the Bronx, New York. The second class refers to the alleged voluntary confession made by the defendant. You must determine whether the witnesses who have testified have told the truth or whether they have willfully falsified their testimony, and whether they are biased or mistaken as to facts.

"Upon you alone rests the responsibility of determining the weight you will give the testimony of the police officers in this case, and it is of supreme importance for you gentlemen to analyze the evidence free from any feeling that you might have against the police department as a whole. Whatever impression you might have as to some of the police officials in this city you must lay aside in considering the testimony of these officers; you must consider whether they are truth-telling officers."

\*\*\*

What was one to make of Eugene MacBride? Born in Scotland, dragged across the ocean as a boy, only to have his mother die, like mine. To end up in the Bronx, as both sides of my family did, just when the borough's last remaining pastures were being paved over, transformed into mazes of hilly, cobblestoned streets lined with narrow houses teeming with immigrants. He didn't have a vocation. There was no mention anywhere of his having had any kind of spouse or romance in his life. When the trial took place, he was thirty-three years old. He'd gone to Fordham. He had drifted from job to job. He'd been the loser brother, dependent on the limited patience and generosity of sisters who had married men of meager means. He may have had a weakness for drink, like everyone in my family. Reading his testimony, it felt like he'd wished to be seen as a gentleman in the eyes of others, and that he had failed. He had to beg for nickels and dimes. He'd been accused, tried, convicted, and sentenced to death for the brutal rape and murder of an eleven-year-old Swedish girl he may never have laid a hand on. The satanic irony of it. The grim American tale it told, of a kind rarely chronicled, stories of the ones who didn't make it, for whom the glory of the Promised Land was a pile of shit.

We drove to my home in Williamstown, known to all the realtors in the area as the Cole Porter estate. It was chilly and damp inside the main house from being shut up for such a long time. Just as Caro had done with my mother's things in the Bronx, Carmen and I gathered what remained of Scarlett's shoes and clothing and stuffed them into heavy-duty garbage bags that we then drove to a collection bin. I was all right with it.

Back on the property we lay in the sun and swam in the pool that I kept maintained each year. I couldn't remember the last time I'd done that there. And I'd never done it feeling so in love. After a bite of lunch in town we came back to the house and retired to the master bedroom. I felt like a damn fool for having spent so much time at the Wheatleigh. In the afternoon we went for another swim.

"What happened at the Institute of Fine Arts?" she asked, draping an arm into the water. "You mentioned something about having enemies."

"It's an extraordinary place, really special, but there were some personality clashes. My fault surely. Some folks there considered me a kind of dinosaur. As I told you in Paris, I've always done my best to avoid jargon and theory when talking about art, and I was ostracized a bit for it. When Scarlett got sick and the position at the Clark opened up, I went for it. Things are much more laid back up here and Williams seemed more like college, as I remember it."

"And is it?"

"Enough. It's a great institution."

We dined at Mezze in Williamstown and ran into a colleague and her female partner. It was good to see them and they could not have been nicer. Back at the house I lit a fire and opened an old bottle of port neither of us liked. We chatted and snuggled on the sofa in front of the hearth and then went upstairs to bed. After we finished making love, I heard Carmen crying in the bathroom. I went to the door and called in.

"Are you all right?" I said, an absurd question in those circumstances.

She didn't reply.

"Can I come in?" I said, as gently as possible.

"No," she said, in a neutral tone.

I got back into bed and waited for her. I prepared myself for just about anything. She came out and got in next to me. I took one of her hands and kissed it.

"I'm sorry," she said.

"You've nothing to be sorry for."

"I'm not used to this," she said, seemingly on the verge of tears again.

"Me neither."

"I suppose I'm scared," she said.

I was about to say "me too" but thought better of it, not wanting to sound like I was trying to make everything about me, like I was competing with her.

"What are you scared of?" I asked instead.

"Of you. Of me. A lot of feelings, you know, have been unlocked all of a sudden."

Our intimacy, intense, was proving cathartic. And though I'd felt from the very start that I knew her, knew her in some deep, fundamental way, a way that transcended her immediate concerns and any possible other entanglements still unclear to me, I also had to accept that some of those ideas on my part might be a self-serving fantasy.

"Whatever those feelings are," I said, "this feels very good to me."

"I guess that's what I'm afraid of."

I took her in my arms. "Don't be. Let's just enjoy it and see where it goes. Don't worry. We're not perfect, but I'm pretty sure we mean well. I certainly do. And I'm mad for you."

I sensed she wanted to tell me something. But she didn't. We lay there like that in silence until she fell asleep. Cool mountain air was coming through the screen, and rather than close the window or go look for a blanket, I carefully got out of bed and lit a fire in the bedroom fireplace. Corru fell asleep by the hearth. Then I took a hot shower and came back to her, kissing her some more. Before falling asleep myself, I found myself thinking of the garbage bags with Scarlett's clothing in them, all mushed together in a rusty green metal container by a convenience store near North Adams. Thousands of dollars of clothes and shoes she had once bought and worn with such delight. I thought I'd been okay with it, but there in bed I felt guilty. And it reminded me of "the bundle," of the clothing that Ingrid Anderson's mother had made for her and stuffed into a bag as well.

Watching Carmen's plane take off from Pittsfield the following day I felt at peace, but also forlorn. I returned to the Wheatleigh and smelled the pillows she'd rested her head upon. At my table for one that night, I texted back and forth with her like all the other idiots I despised for doing the very same thing during dinner.

I finished the Géricault article in two days and sent it off to Paris. I hired movers who went through the house with me, tagging everything I wanted to give away or put into storage. By the following day the place was virtually empty. I arranged for a contractor to paint the interiors white. I wanted it to be cleaned out, to be transformed into a fresh canvas that either I could put up for sale or that we could do up together some day as we pleased.

I flew to Boston, this time staying at the Charles, a pretty awful hotel. Carmen spent the night with me and during the following day, as she taught her classes and worked in her lab, I crossed the river and went to the Museum of Fine Arts and then to the Isabella Stewart Gardner museum, where I hadn't been for years. The recent Renzo Piano wing underwhelmed me, and the house itself, though charming for the chaotic distribution of its artwork, was darker and drearier than I remembered. The majority of the people visiting both institutions were frumpy and depressing to be around. The contrast with my memories of what it had been like to visit the MOMA and the Metropolitan and the Frick in my teens and early twenties was stark.

Carmen accepted my invitation to visit Caro in Southampton with me as soon as her term finished, and I returned to Lenox and Williamstown to wrap up some things of my own. On my last night there I walked the grounds at the house with Corru. Night fell as we strolled. I paused before a tall and thick Norwegian pine. My first reaction was to enjoy a sense of property. Though Cole and Linda Porter had once inhabited these grounds, I felt the tree and the earth it grew from were mine. It was a lord of the manor moment, infused with sentimentality about time and its passage, how I'd first come there with Scarlett as opposed to where I was then in my life. But the tree and the grounds had known many owners, for almost three centuries, and before that it had simply been part of the woods and meadows the indigenous inhabitants had hunted through. It would surely know many more owners as time progressed, after I sold it or after I was gone.

I closed the house and drove back to Lenox for a late dinner at a wine bar in town where I got half tanked on a very good Bandol rosé from the Domaine Tempier. When I got up in the middle of the night to pee and brush my teeth for a second time, I found Corru in the bathroom where, unable to contain himself, he'd retired to do his business. It's what I deserved for giving him some of the shrimp I had with the wine. He looked up at me as if to ask for forgiveness and it brought me to tears. I don't know why. I cleaned everything and picked him up and brought him back to bed with me. He was okay with me doing that by then. He wasn't afraid anymore. I watched him fall asleep and thought back to the damp little house in Extremadura where I had first seen him.

## 30

**Beauregard L. Harrison:** "I have been a photographer for the past twelve years. At the request of the District Attorney's office I went to St. Michael's Cemetery on Long Island and took this photograph. I also developed the negative."

**Prosecuting Attorney:** "Gentlemen of the jury, in admitting this photograph in evidence, the District Attorney offers it solely for the purpose of showing the nature of the character and place where the alleged wounds were inflicted upon the deceased; it is only offered for that purpose; and in viewing the photograph you must not permit anything that appears in the photograph to tend to inflame your judgment against the person on trial, it is not admitted for any such purpose, that is, whether the child was a beautiful child or not, that is immaterial."

**The Court:** "The defendant is presumed to be innocent until he is proved to be guilty. The presumption rests with him throughout the case until the moment when the jury is convinced from the proof submitted to them that the defendant is guilty of the crimes charged. Then the presumption of innocence is destroyed."

**Mr. Tannenbaum:** "I respectfully ask Your Honor to charge that the prosecution has failed to prove any specific motive for the defendant to have killed the deceased."

**The Court:** "I so charge."

**Mr. Tannenbaum:** "I will ask Your Honor to also charge that there is no proof in this case that the motive for the alleged killing of the deceased was the concealment of the crime of rape."

**The Court:** "That is for the jury to determine."

**Mr. Tannenbaum:** "I ask Your Honor to charge that if the jury finds that the confession was forced from the mind of the defendant by the flattery of hope, or by torture or because of fear produced by threats, they must reject it."

**The Court:** "I so charge."

**The Court:** "Gentlemen of the jury, you may retire."

## 31

I flew Carmen to Pittsfield again and picked her up in the G-Wagon. After six months sitting around shrouded in a Lenox garage, it needed a workout. We were about to drive down to New York and I was reluctant to risk putting the forty-year-old Citroën through its paces on such a journey. I wended my way to the Taconic Parkway and cruised south. Up there it was a beautiful highway, but it got increasingly narrow and filled with cars as we neared the city. I clung, as I often do just about everywhere now, to outdated fantasies of the terrain, imagining it as I pretended it had been during my youth. While Carmen described more facets of her childhood in Madrid, and what Spain had been like in the late 1980s, summering as a little girl in Galicia, I listened happily while retrofitting the Berkshires and Dutchess County.

I erased all the strip malls and most of the people who lived there now. I banished all the wealthy, puritanical exercise freaks. I reintroduced farmers who cut their own wood and read the *Saturday Evening Post*, Rockwell-like figures who pumped gas, doctors who made house calls, dairies that delivered milk in thick bottles, women in tweed coats out walking their dogs, girls in summer dresses mad about horses, Korean War and Vietnam veterans skilled with Zippo lighters. I gave everyone a foxy sex life and a favorite book. I brought back movies with Audrey Hepburn or Katharine Hepburn, Gary Cooper and William Holden. It was ridiculous and therapeutic.

Carmen spoke a bit more about her father. She had tenuous memories of him teaching her how to swim off the beaches of the Cíes Islands. Hearing him swear in Italian when he got angry. Putting her to bed and singing Russian lullabies. She mentioned a portrait he did of her when she was five that she kept at her place in Cambridge and that she promised to show me. As we sped by exits for FDR's Hyde Park estate I heard about her early crushes and Madrid's teenage disco world.

Then, as we started passing exits for Yonkers, her attention came back to me and she convinced me to man up and drive through Highbridge. I did it to please her, to demonstrate I was not as neurotic as in fact I am. What impressed me most, after getting off the highway and grappling with streets that were common in my most unsettling dreams, but difficult to find in real life, was how different everything looked while managing to remain creepily familiar, the persistence of the avenue names and most of the buildings lining them. The persistence of bricks. In the 1970s and '80s Highbridge went downhill and only took an upturn in the '90s when crime rates began to go down and the sturdy apartment buildings and two-family homes proved attractive to a growing African American and Hispanic middle class.

I refused to stop and get out in front of what had been our apartment building on Undercliff Avenue. I'm glad to say she found this amusing. The front of the building was no longer grand, but otherwise it looked to be in fair shape. Being there again was difficult to process and I distracted myself by talking a blue streak.

In between what had been our building and another similar to it half a block farther south, just before a dark granite arch of the Washington Bridge, there had been two tenements left over from an even earlier era. When I'd driven by some years before they were still there, just as grim looking as I remembered. In our building and in the other one like it, mostly progressive Jewish families had lived along with some Irish folk like mine. But the two tenements had housed humbler tenants. I most remember the Rossetti family. I befriended one of their sons, Ricardo, who got into fights and always had a runny nose. Sometimes his mother had me over for a meal. The stairwells and hallways smelled of garbage and canned tomato sauce. Mrs. Rossetti, clearly pretty once upon a time, had a ravaged look by then. There was an older daughter famous for being "fast" and an older son who often got arrested. The only reason these memories, images, and smells remained active in my brain was because it was Ricardo who first told me my mother had died. On that day with Carmen the tenements were gone. They'd been replaced with a new residential apartment building that was not especially pleasing to look at but was probably considered desirable in the neighborhood for being modern.

I drove us to the beginning of Ogden Avenue where there used to be a pharmacy and, a bit farther along, the movie theater where I sat through numerous triple features as a child, Abbott and Costello films and Westerns. After five minutes of driving by bodegas and check-cashing businesses, beauty salons, and some prison-like public schools, we arrived at the scene of the crime, the stretch of Ogden Avenue where I'd played and stayed with my paternal grandparents, where the Colossi barber shop had been, where MacBride had sat on that wall, and where Ingrid Anderson was raped and strangled to death.

I parked the G-Wagon and we got out—at Carmen's insistence. The people strolling on the sidewalk smiled at us or ignored us, going about their business. A great shock hit me immediately. Of all the buildings on both sides of the street, only two had disappeared: 1075 and 1077, the buildings where my grandparents had lived, where my father and his brothers were born and grew up, where Ingrid's family, MacBride, and the Conlans had lived.

Where once those houses with their matching granite stoops had stood, there was now a vacant lot filled with weeds, shredded plastic bags, and shards of broken stone. What had happened? Was it karma, sheer coincidence, or had their disappearance been connected in any way to the crime? The latter option was the most implausible because the crime took place in 1916 and I had known those buildings long after. But it was still uncanny. Carmen was nevertheless convinced there had to be a connection. She asked the owner of a nearby store when the buildings had been destroyed, speaking to him in Spanish, but the man had no idea.

What was still there was the fire station across the way. It was now designated EMS Station 17, and though it had undergone various alterations, its basic structure remained intact and a modern fire truck was parked within it at the ready. I crossed the street and asked one of the firemen about the fate of 1075/77 and he thought they'd been razed sometime in the 1980s. I thanked him and crossed back to where Carmen was standing by the chain link fence. I remembered what the janitor, Albert Boulder, had said at the trial: *I am the janitor of the premises 1075 and 1077 Ogden Avenue. They are double tenement houses, five stories each, with ten families in each house. Under these houses there are basements.* I wondered if the basements were still there. I wondered if they'd been filled in with earth and debris, or had they just been covered over when the buildings came down? Whatever the case, there it was, not fifteen feet in front of us—the exact spot on this planet where Ingrid had been murdered. The stoops where she and Edwin and my father and his brothers and Gino Colossi played, and where I had played half a century later, were gone. The room where I'd eaten butter and raisins with my grandmother, she who'd been born in County Clare, was gone. But the basements, in one fashion or the other, were probably still there.

The Valiunas saloon and the Colossi barbershop were long gone as well, and driving around the corner onto Woodycrest Avenue we stopped in front of what had been the Judge's house, where the dream I had in Paris had taken place, where my mother had lived until she married my father, and where I had spent many nights sleeping in what had been her room. It was painted a different color and had been repaired. In fact, all of Woodycrest Avenue shone with renewal. Many of the fine wooden homes had been renovated. New cars were parked in front of them. Down the hill, even the scary orphanage edifice had been steam-cleaned and repurposed.

Rather than pushing on and heading out to Southampton as planned, I called Caro and told her we'd arrive the following day. I was reeling from the Bronx tour and suggested to Carmen that we spend the night in the city living it up a little.

# - 32 -

At 4:50 p.m., the jury returned to the courtroom.

**The Clerk:** "Have you agreed upon a verdict?"

**The Foreman:** "We have."

**The Clerk:** "How say you, do you find the defendant at the bar guilty or not guilty?"

**The Foreman:** "We find him guilty as charged in the indictment of murder in the first degree and guilty as charged in the indictment of rape in the first degree."

**Mr. Tannenbaum:** "May it please Your Honor, I respectfully move to set aside the verdict of the jury and ask for a new trial upon the grounds, first, that the verdict is contrary to law; second, that the verdict is clearly against the evidence and the weight of the evidence; and thirdly, that the Court at the trial admitted illegal and improper evidence against the defendant's objections."

**The Court:** "Motion denied. When will you be ready for sentence?"

**Mr. Tannenbaum:** "I think Your Honor ought to give me about a week; say a week from today."

I'd felt like a stranger in my own city for some time. In the early 1990s, Scarlett and I moved out of Bunky's Fifth Avenue "palazzo" after buying a loft on Spring Street. There was a weekend phenomenon back then everyone referred to as the invasion of the Bridge & Tunnel people, revelers that drove into lower Manhattan weekend nights gumming up the streets, restaurants, and clubs to such an extent that many from the crowd we hung out with stayed in or fled to their country homes. It had actually been another incentive for taking the job at the Clark Museum.

After Scarlett died and I returned to New York on visits, it felt as if the bridge-and-tunnel brigade had taken over. They'd somehow made a lot of money working in the city all that time, commuting from New Jersey and Queens and Long Island City, and had managed to buy bits and pieces of Manhattan. Every time I went to a restaurant, even to the two or three that survived from what I consider a golden age, they were filled with these people; young, well paid, wearing patterned sweaters and awful shoes, what I might call a Fort Lee look.

Diehards always consider "their" New York to be the cool and stylish one as they gaze upon arrivistes with horror. But I have to say, the New York I grew up in, and knew young adulthood in, and then kept living in as an absurdly rich and essentially useless man, really was much cooler and more stylish than it is now. Now it's *only* about money and real estate, celebs and crass social climbing, in a town that continues to be hard-edged, tiring, and uncomfortable, and that is still filled with black plastic garbage bags piled by the gutters every morning. I just couldn't see myself living there anymore. I carried the New York that had been mine around with me, safe and undisturbed. Mine still had Bonwit Teller and Best & Co., Rumplemayer's and the Women's Exchange, Schrafft's on Madison Avenue, Aggie's downtown, and the Cedar Tavern on University Place. It had the Second Avenue Deli when it was still on Second Avenue.

I checked us in to the Bowery Hotel and got my favorite suite on the top floor with the large terrace and outdoor shower. We had dinner downstairs at Gemma at a corner table out of the way. A film star was there with a small coterie, all of them dressed idiotically in black, along with the usual crowd of ambitious youths, all of them with their phones out on the table. But the lighting was appealing, the food and wine good, and the waiters friendly and discreet.

"I've an idea," Carmen said after we toasted with two glasses of Brunello. "Why not buy that lot?"

"On Ogden Avenue?" I knew immediately what she was referring to.

"Yes."

"To do what with?"

"You could rebuild the houses exactly as they were, on the outside, but turn the inside into something else, like a foundation or something."

"A foundation."

"Yes," she said, "you could call it something like the Ingrid Anderson Foundation for Children, and the place could provide counseling or something like that."

"Why didn't I think of this?"

"Because the whole area gives you the heebie-jeebies, but it might be a good thing to do, fitting somehow. I mean, you lived in that actual building, right?"

"My grandparents and my father and his brothers did," I said, "but yes, I spent time there."

"It might be good for you and constitute a public service. You could probably afford it, no?"

"It's a great idea," I said. "I wouldn't even have to go and see it. I could just plan it and fund it."

"If you'd like."

Back in the room she admired the hotel stationery with its Bill the Butcher iconography and I told her how when I was around twelve and beginning to have crushes on girls I'd take stationery from hotels, the fancier the better, and use them to write my love letters. I would be too ashamed to send them from the Bronx and so I'd wait until I got to Manhattan before posting them.

We showered together out on the terrace before going to bed. We stood there soaping each other, looking at the rooftops across the way and down to the new Trade Center skyscraper. Despite all my grumbling about Manhattan's decline and fall, it was a moment I did not plan to forget.

After she fell asleep, I read the end of the trial transcript.

# - 34 -

Thursday, October 31, 1916.

**Mr. Northshire (for the District Attorney):** "If the Court please, the People move for judgment in the case of People against Eugene J. MacBride."

**The Clerk:** "Eugene J. MacBride, have you any cause to show why judgment of death not now be pronounced against you?"

**Mr. Tannenbaum:** "I move for an arrest of judgment upon the same grounds specified by me at the time of the rendition of the verdict."

**The Court:** "Motion denied."

**Mr. Tannenbaum:** "I cannot say anything else. The law imposes upon Your Honor your duty."

**The Court:** "Eugene J. MacBride, the judgment of the court is that you, for the murder and rape in the first degree of one Ingrid Anderson, whereof you are convicted, be you and hereby, sentenced to punishment of death; and it is ordered that within ten days after this day's session of the Court that the Sheriff of the County of New York deliver you to the Agent and Warden of the State Prison of the State of New York at Sing Sing, where you shall be kept in solitary confinement, until the week beginning on the tenth day of December 1916, and upon some day within the week so appointed the said Agent and Warden of the State Prison at Sing Sing is commanded to do execution upon you in the mode and manner prescribed by the laws of the State of New York."

- 35 -

I told Carmen about MacBride's verdict and sentence over breakfast. It sort of put a pall on a good part of the day. Before heading
out to Southampton, I left Corru with a dog sitter at the hotel and
made the mistake of taking Carmen uptown to see Bunky's place at
820 Fifth, the one Dirk Salisbury gave me so much grief about. I
hadn't been for a long time and thought to show it to her before I
would probably follow her suggestion and put it up for sale.
Regardless of how things might pan out between us, her notion that
I free myself of it seemed a healthy thing to do—but I should have
gone on my own.

The elevator opened directly onto a wide entrance hall that ran
parallel to the avenue below. Stepping into the apartment, we were
greeted by a minor but very beautiful work by Francisco de Zurbarán.
It was one of his many representations of the Immaculate Conception.
Carmen was shocked to see it there and was taken with it. It gave me
pleasure to watch her marvel at it, especially since I'd always found
it a tad depressing, associating it with Bunky's Catholic upbringing
that, like mine, had done considerable damage.

"Just think," she said, "it was painted in Sevilla four hundred
years ago, and here it is in your apartment!"

"Bunky's mother bought it at auction," I said. "She was very old
school and resented the presence of Bill Paley's kingdom two floors
below. When you stepped out of the elevator at the Paleys', there was

Picasso's *Boy with a Horse*. This was her Catholic reply. Bunky had a love-hate relationship with it and when he was drunk, which was often, he'd stand here in front of it spewing forth streams of profanity."

Both floors of my apartment were a homage to the 1970s, when hostesses like Peggy Bancroft, C. Z. Guest, and Babe Paley made the Upper East Side their fiefdom. Billy Baldwin had decorated it originally and no one had bothered to change anything since. Thick gold drapes framed the many windows looking down at the park. Pineapple-shaped lamps graced tables placed at either end of deep, comfortable, pink and white sofas. Art and photography books popular in the period competed for space on coffee tables strewn with Steuben ashtrays and monogrammed cigarette cases. Small white porcelain monkeys rested on one of the mantels. Framed photographs of family members, long deceased, adorned side tables.

"None of the other works of art hold a candle to what the Paleys had downstairs," I continued as we walked about. "Their living room walls were plastered with Gauguins. I spent a lot of time there in my teens. I was close to their daughter. Truman Capote was over a lot, dishing gossip that kept everyone enthralled. Paley was nervous and jumpy and always tasting everyone's food at restaurants. Ba and Carter Burden would wander in and out like royalty making the other siblings uncomfortable with envy. Whenever you left a room for any reason, all of the cushions were re-fluffed, and all the ashtrays were cleaned by the time you returned. It was a very uptight and weird household but at the same time you felt special being there."

She didn't say anything. We toured the bedrooms on the upper level. Thankfully the closets and bureaus and medicine cabinets were empty. The TVs were old Zeniths. The phones were made of thick black plastic and had push button dial pads. In the library off the living room downstairs there was a mirrored bar and a couch and various comfortable chairs covered in red velvet with numerous needlepointed cushions depicting pugs and horses. Others had phrases embroidered on them, aiming to amuse. One that Carmen picked up read EAT, DRINK & REMARRY.

It was somehow fitting that the room in which she chose to speak with me was the servants' TV room off the kitchen, near the door where deliveries were made and where the trash was taken out. We sat in two upholstered chairs that were the worse for wear, frayed about the edges with yellowing antimacassars on the verge of disintegration. The chairs faced a TV that had a lace doily on top of it supporting a large rabbit-ear antenna. I had only vague memories of the immigrant employees who had spent large amounts of time in that room, people who worked for Bunky's parents and then for Scarlett and me until we moved downtown. They had sat in those same chairs, night after night during the Kennedy and Johnson and Nixon administrations, after their many chores were done, watching American TV.

Carmen sat us down and I suddenly remembered a night when I woke and found that Scarlett was not at my side. She was not in the bathroom either. I looked for her and finally found her there in that room curled up and asleep in the chair Carmen was sitting in, the TV flickering, showing an old film, the original 1949 version of *Mighty Joe Young*. I never asked her why she went down there. I covered her with a blanket and sat in the other chair, the one I was sitting in that morning, and watched the rest of the movie.

"Why are we here?" Carmen said.

"I wanted you to see it. Just like I wanted you to see the house in Williamstown."

"But it was me who wanted to see the house in Williamstown," she said. "I didn't ask to come here."

"I know," I said. "I'm sorry. I wanted you to see it because I'm thinking of finally selling it."

"I think you should," she said. "But I didn't need to see it for that. You could have made that decision on your own. I've nothing to do with this. You keep these homes like they were tombs."

"You're right."

"All this stuff about the Paleys and Truman Capote and Bunky and his family and your ex-wife, all of the New York social history you find so colorful and that you appear to be so nostalgic about, is a little depressing to me. I've nothing to do with it. It's like leafing through an old issue of *Look* magazine at a garage sale. I know it's been part of your life, and to the extent it interests me at all, it's because of that, because you interest me. But. I don't know. This place really bums me out."

I looked down at the black and white tiles covering the floor.

"Then maybe going out to visit with Caro might not be such a great idea."

"No. That does appeal to me. I'm happy to do that. She's alive. She's actually your family. She helped bring you up. But this is something else. I'm not jealous. It's not that."

"I get it," I said.

"Perhaps I shouldn't have pushed you to go through the Bronx yesterday. I mean, we were happily on our way out to Long Island."

"I'm glad you urged me to do it," I said. "Well—glad is not the word exactly—but it proved to be a good reality check. Just like coming back here is turning out to be. Come on," I said, standing up and extending my hand for her to take. "Let's go."

As we stepped back into the elevator, she said, "Whatever you end up doing, keep the Zurbarán."

## 36

The land southeast of Main Street in the Southampton I came to as a newborn was mostly dedicated to potato farms owned by the Halsey and Burnett families. The rich built their homes along South Main Street, Gin Lane, First Neck Lane, and Great Plains and Ox Pasture Roads. The Beach Club was constructed opposite the southern end of Lake Agawam adjacent to St. Andrew's Dune Church. The Meadow Club was put up a bit farther west, set back from the beach next to Coopers Neck Pond where Meadow Lane turns into Dune Road.

When I was little, I was told that Lake Agawam had no bottom, that divers descended into it and never returned, that it was connected to the ocean by an underground cavern. This explained why during hurricanes the strange gray and cappuccino-like foam that washed up on the beach appeared as well about the southern border of the lake. On one occasion, after a hurricane, I watched ocean waves break over the dunes and merge with the lake.

The women who worked for us there when I was little, who cooked and cleaned the house and sometimes took care of me, were Shinnecock Indians. One of them took me fishing sometimes in ponds on the reservation. I remember the thin bamboo poles, the little hooks that hurt my fingers, and the small sun perch we caught. I remember the pull of the fish when it grabbed the hook, the sudden tug, the thrill and the sadness of it. The woman would gut them and bring them back to her house to fry and we ate them with untoasted slices of Wonder Bread and heated cans of beans with bits of bacon in them. Sitting at the folding aluminum table, holding my fork, I felt invincible.

The Judge took me deep sea fishing for bluefish and striped bass in cabin cruisers rented from the Montauk docks. From the beach in front of our house at Fair Lea, he and my uncles, but never my father, would surf-cast. The lures they used were wooden and colorful with metal joints and multiple hooks and they made a satisfying splash clearing the waves fifty or sixty yards out. What they mostly caught were sea robins, sand sharks, and skate.

I remember Dusty Miller and the papyrus-like long grass growing on the ocean side of the dunes and the wild rose hip and beach plum shrubs growing on the land side. I remember the sandy path we took to access the beach, hot at times, that went from the lawn at Fair Lea up through the shrubs. In early September during the hurricane season the beach plums would be ripe for picking and back in the kitchen the Judge would drive Aunt Jane mad making a great mess—the boiling of the berries, the bags of white sugar, straining everything through yards of gauze, adding the pectin and melting the wax to cap each jar before fastening down the tin lids that later would only pry open with a knife blade.

I remember the milkman and his truck and the man who cut our lawns, a handsome tattooed vet who drove an oily green Ford tractor while wearing aviator sunglasses, who always had a pack of Lucky Strikes tucked in a sleeve. I loved the poppy seed buns and jelly donuts from the Hampton Bakery, Crutchley's donut holes in powdered sugar that we got after buying the newspapers at Jack's. The stores along Main Street: Hobbyland, Herricks and Hildreths, Hildegard Peter, Saks Fifth Avenue, and Silver's next to a pharmacy that had a soda fountain. Shep Miller on Job's Lane, and Peck &

Peck, and Jax, and Lillywhites that smelled of new bicycle tires for the English racers sold there, and the Act IV ice cream parlor run by Stan and Clyde, a theatrically gay couple from Florida. The grassy square with the piled cannon balls, Shippy's and his pretty wife who often had a black eye, the Windmill Diner where locals went, the movie theater up the hill when it only had one screen.

I remember Mr. Dox who ran the gymnastics classes at the Beach Club, and Artie and Sven, the Norwegian lifeguards who put out the barrels at the beginning of each summer and who migrated with the members to Palm Beach and the Everglades Club during the winter season. I remember having lunch with Mrs. William Randolph Hearst, Millicent, the former dance hall girl, and her sister Anita, when I used a finger bowl for the first time. She asked me what I wanted to be when I grew up and I told her I wanted to be a painter, and she replied, "Study Rubens. Study Rubens."

And I remember fixating on the young Mrs. Dan Topping's beautiful breasts as she basted them with Bain de Soleil, not minding me because I was so little, and then winking at me before closing her eyes and lying back down in the sun. I remember my father hitting fungo on the lawn at Fair Lea using actual New York Yankee baseballs. I remember my mother alive there. And I remember the summer after she died, and then the summer five years later when we began to live with Caro at her house.

But I didn't share any of these recollections with Carmen that day. We drove out without stopping, talking about American and European politics, her favorite places in Spain, and a bit more about what might be done with the vacant lots on Ogden Avenue. Then she looked up Sing Sing on her phone and learned that the electric chair used there was called "Old Sparky." She looked that up as well and read me the following Wikipedia entry:

In 1887, New York State established a committee to determine a new, more humane system of execution to replace hanging. Alfred P. Southwick, a member of the committee, developed the idea of putting electric current through a device after hearing about how relatively painlessly and quickly a drunken man died after touching exposed power lines. As Southwick was a dentist accustomed to performing procedures on sitting subjects, his electrical device appeared in the form of a chair.

On June 4, 1888, Governor David B. Hill authorized the introduction of the electric chair. It was first used two years later when William Kemmler became the first person in the world to be executed by electricity at Auburn Prison, Auburn, New York on August 6, 1890.

"Old Sparky" was first used at Sing Sing prison in 1891. The chair was situated in a purpose-built building known as the Death House, which was a prison within the high-security Sing Sing prison. The block, which had its own hospital, kitchen, visiting room, and exercise yard, had twenty-four single cells plus an additional three cells for condemned women. A chamber where a prisoner spent their last day was nicknamed the "Dance Hall." A corridor, known as the "Last Mile," connected the anteroom to the execution chamber.

Executions at Sing Sing were traditionally carried out at 11 p.m. on Thursdays. Condemned prisoners would be brought into the execution room escorted by seven guards and the prison chaplain. Already waiting in the room would be the warden of Sing Sing, the state electrician, two doctors and twelve state appointed witnesses. After the condemned prisoner was strapped into the chair and the electrodes attached, the warden would step forward and read out the final decision on the sentence. The prisoner would be asked for any last words or for a benediction.

With a signal, the execution would then begin. Witnesses would leave once both doctors had confirmed that death had occurred.

In its seventy-five years of operation, a total of 695 men and women were executed by the electric chair in New York State—614 at Sing Sing alone. From 1914, all executions were conducted at Sing Sing prison using "Old Sparky." Eddie Mays would become the last person to be executed on August 15, 1963. Two years later New York State abolished capital punishment.[1]

---

1       Wikipeia, s.v. "Old Sparky," last modified March 8, 2021, 18:34, https://en.wikipedia.org/wiki/Old_Sparky#New_York

## 37

After passing the Shinnecock Golf Club I got off Route 27 onto Tuckahoe Lane and drove to Hill Street and then onto Halsey Neck Lane to Dune Road. I drove her by the Beach Club and then I took her into the Fair Lea driveway to show her the house we had for so many summers. The property had been subdivided since then and there were new houses where once there'd only been the great lawn leading to the beach. Everything looked smaller. Chastened by what had happened at the apartment in New York, I kept my commentary to a minimum. Then we took Gin Lane to Old Town Road and on to Wickapogue until we came to the Cuddihy-Woodward compound.

On the portion of their land nearest to the driveway's main gate, Caro's nieces, nephews, and their children had broken up a good deal of the estate building their own cottages, with swimming pools and access lanes. Caro lived in the original house, what had been her parents' house. It was by far the biggest and grandest house, the one closest to the dunes with the most land around it. Many a Kennedy, FDR once, Al Smith, numerous children, and various pink-bellied New York cardinals from St. Patrick's had splashed around in its swimming pool. Away from the pool there was a flower and vegetable garden and then the large garage where Edwin Anderson had lived and where I had stayed in exile during my senior year of high school.

Caro was waiting for us on the front porch. I hadn't seen her since Thanksgiving. That past Christmas I'd selfishly stayed away. I was with someone in Morocco, a liaison that ended up going nowhere. She wore a pair of white sharkskin slacks, navy Belgian loafers with black trim, and a quince-toned Mexican shirt. Her hair was pulled back into a smooth white ponytail. She thought Carmen was beautiful and told her so and then told her I hadn't brought another woman to meet her for as long as she could remember, "And that is a *very* long time." Once inside I put Corru in her lap and gained some extra points there as well. I introduced Carmen to the maids and the cook, all of them Irish. While I walked Corru around the grounds, Caro took Carmen by the arm to give her a tour of the house.

I chose a guest room for us I didn't normally use, a bigger room than the one I usually stayed in. It was at the very far end of the upstairs hall, as far from Caro's as possible so that we'd have maximum privacy. The bathroom had an old standalone cast iron tub with lion claw feet, and we could see the ocean from bed.

On the following day I drove into town alone to get some things and on the way back I parked by Old Town Beach and made some calls. I spoke with a lawyer I use and to the woman who handled most of my real estate transactions. I asked her to put the apartment at 820 Fifth on the market and to look into buying the lot on Ogden Avenue. In the afternoon we had tea with Caro and then took a walk down the beach with Corru and went for a swim in the ocean. Drying off in the afternoon sun, Carmen told me she'd had a rather intense conversation while I'd been doing my errands. I was pleased that Caro felt so at ease with her, said so, and was about to go in the water again when Carmen said, "She told me things I promised not to repeat."

"Really," I said, stopping and coming back.

"I was shocked, because I've just met her, but I guess it was something she was looking to get off her chest."

"Well, she's a perceptive lady who's been around a long time, and I suspect she knows you're a keeper with a capital K."

"That's sweet of you," Carmen said. "She put it differently. She said she'd not had a proper woman to talk with for a long time, that all her friends were dead. She said that when you mentioned Edwin Anderson on the phone many memories flooded back that, as a good Catholic girl, she had repressed for a long time. What she told me was a bit like a confession, a ribald one. You know, the way the elderly just stop caring sometimes about certain kinds of propriety, and just tell it like it was."

"I'm all ears."

"It started when she said, 'I noticed he brought you to see the room over the garage last evening, where he lived on his own the year he finally finished high school.' That's right, I said to her. 'You were up there for some time,' she said, and I must have blushed, because then she said, 'I bet he took your clothes off.'"

"She actually said that?"

"She did."

"I should have warned you. For the past decade or so all kinds of unfiltered stuff comes out of her mouth when you least expect it. What did you say?"

"I said, 'He did.'"

"My god."

"And then she said, 'What *is* it about that room?'"

"Wow."

"That was nothing compared with what came next."

"Anything to do with Edwin?"

"Yes. But you can't give even the smallest hint, ever, that I told you this."

"I won't."

"She made me promise not to tell you until after she was dead."

171

"I understand."

"She had an affair with him."

I stared at her, then turned my head and stared at the ocean.

"Are you sure you want to hear this?" Carmen said.

"Yes."

"It's a bit kinky."

I looked back at her again.

"My stepmother had a kinky affair with Ingrid Anderson's brother? You don't think I want to hear about that?"

She laughed. "Okay, okay."

"How kinky?"

"She wasn't overly explicit and I'm not sure I understood everything, but she was with him often, before and during the time she was married to your father. It was an important relationship to her. She said that in a perfect world she would have married him."

"Maybe that's why Edwin left," I said. "Maybe my father found out and fired him."

"Not according to her," Carmen said. "She told me he and your father always got along, and she told me what she told you, that Edwin left when his mother got ill and wanted to go back to Sweden, late in life, and he felt obliged to take her and care for her there, until she passed away, and after that, according to Caro, he stayed there as well. He never returned to the United States."

I was looking out at the ocean again as she said all this. Waves ideal for riding were rolling in. Just before they crested light shone through them.

"Go on," I said.

"She said she had certain tastes, certain proclivities she discovered and fantasized about, and could never tell anyone about, including your father because he was, in her words, excessively normal. And there was this one day when she came back from riding a horse she had."

"Rocio," I said.

"Rocio?"

"That was the horse's name. I used to ride her too."

"It's a Spanish word. Do you know what it means?"

"No idea."

"It means 'dew.' Anyway, she came back from riding and got into a conversation with Edwin while he was changing the oil or doing something with one of your family cars. She said she told him she felt bad because the horse had misbehaved at some point, refusing to do what she wanted, and she'd given it some whacks with her riding crop and she felt very guilty about it and thought she should be thrashed herself—and that when she said that—he looked at her in a certain way."

"Whoa."

"And that's how it started," she said.

"With a riding crop?"

"She said it drove her crazy. That she'd go up to his room and bend over the couch so that he could whip her behind, not viciously she said, but not gently either. And then she would get him to touch her, you know, like fondle her, immediately afterward, and that it gave her tremendous orgasms."

"Whoa."

"She said that undressing for bed at night she sometimes had welts on her bottom, and that your father never noticed."

"Jesus."

"She said she got him to do other things to her too."

"Like what?"

"I didn't press her. She was excited as she was telling me, but then she got embarrassed and pulled back. She made the sign of the cross, clammed up, and had me swear not to ever tell anyone, especially you."

"Jesus."

173

"And then she asked about our sex life."

"What is she on?"

"She said Edwin didn't have any girlfriends from what she could tell, or boyfriends either, but that they gave each other a lot of pleasure and that after he left he wrote her letters to a PO box she opened in town here and in New York just for that purpose."

"I can't believe it," I said. "I wonder if he ever spoke to her about Ingrid."

"She said that after he left, she used to go to his room to get away from everyone, until you moved in, and that she found the riding crop one day hanging in his closet. He'd left it for her. She still has it."

"So, she was in love with him."

"She didn't say that. Just that they had a special bond, something she had never found with anyone else."

"I'm astonished."

"She's an amazing woman."

"You have these fixed ideas about people," I said, "and then . . . I feel bad for my father."

"She said she didn't think he knew, or if he suspected anything, he was okay with it, because it never came up."

"Who knows?"

# - 38 -

820 Fifth was assessed and put on the market. The empty lot on Ogden Avenue was available at a reasonable cost. The permits to build replicas of what had been 1075 and 1077, while allowing their interiors to be connected for multipurpose use, would require a lot of paperwork, but it was doable. I told my lawyers to go ahead and I phoned a small architectural firm I trusted and told them to find plans and pictures of how the buildings originally looked. At the very least it would prevent the construction of another anodyne apartment building.

I took Carmen to the Beach Club and ran into friends I'd known since I was a boy. It always took a few seconds to make the adjustment from the way I had them fixed in my mind, from how they had looked many years before, and I'm sure the same thing happened to them upon seeing me. The club, encumbered by all manner of environmental regulations since my youth, had continued to steadily neuterize itself, making it a "safer," more practical place for its members. It had more personality during my tenure there. The pool had a high and low diving board. I don't recall there being a lifeguard. There were no signs listing do's and don'ts. Across from the shallow end, gracing the bottom of the façade of the "big cafeteria," there'd been a small fountain where the water came out of a lion's mouth. The "little cafeteria" was relaxed and open and served you in your bathing suit; delicious hamburgers and pieces of pie and chocolate layer cake. I remember being wrapped in a towel after hours of riding waves, the taste of the burger mixing with the scent of ocean water in my sinuses. There was no fine print on the menu about allergies or gluten. Members drank and smoked. Nobody wore clothing with brand name labels except for the little alligators on Lacoste polo shirts. For me, the definitive decline of the club coincided with the summer when I noticed people wearing shirts with the Ralph Lauren logo on them. It was life imitating art, Ralph Lifshitz from the Bronx, like me, getting the real bluebloods to buy into his fantasy of what their culture was like.

And of course there were no cell phones, so it was normal to hear amusing, richly phrased conversation. There was a feeling back then that the members, no matter how conservative and superficially straitlaced, were into love affairs and fooling around. All the changes, physical and sociological, that had taken place bothered me, but I kept my mouth shut about it and we had a nice day at the beach chatting with buddies for whom art history and structural biology were so alien they weren't worth mentioning. We had lunch outside by the bar, littlenecks on the half shell with a bad chardonnay improved with lots of ice. We sat in the same little corner, now Sanforized, where my father and Caro had been introduced.

We preferred staying at home, swimming in the pool, and in the ocean in front of the house. But one morning toward the end of our stay Caro expressed a wish to go to the club, where she hadn't shown her face for many summers. We helped her into her own car, a beautifully preserved Mercedes coupe from the 1960s, and drove her there. We got her up the front stairs where decades earlier she'd posed so many times for Irving Cantor, the Eastern European freelance photographer with a thick accent who hung out at the bottom of the steps all day every summer. We got her up to the pool level, and then up the second flight of stairs, settling her in a chair on the veranda facing the ocean. Many of the most elderly members stopped by to chat. She seemed to really enjoy herself. She held on to Carmen's arm much of the time, giving her a running commentary about who was who, each tale spiced up with its darkest and most scandalous backstory. I would have killed to record it. Carmen would wink at me now and then and I fell in love with her all over again, grateful for her poise and patience, and I resolved to find a way for Caro to get to the club more often.

So it was a surprise when, having drinks at home that evening, she declared it to have been a perfect day, just as she had hoped, but that she would not be going back there again. For dinner we had her and my favorite dishes, a green salad and rack of lamb with mint jelly and mashed new potatoes with a side of Irish soda bread and lots of butter. I opened two bottles of a 2005 Romanée-Conti. She regaled us with stories about my father, some of them new to me, and stories about her father, the man she loved more than any other, who had probably spanked her too. When Carmen asked her about her mother she pretended not to hear. We kidded her about Javier the gardener, who only the week before had run off with a maid who worked for one of our cousins down the road.

We—all three of us tipsy—helped her up to her room and Carmen stayed with her as the nurse got her ready for bed. Carmen told me the last thing Caro said to her before she left the room was that we should stay together and never leave each other and that she had tears in her eyes when she said it. She relayed this to me as we got into bed.

While she had been with Caro in her room, I'd gone back downstairs and outside with Corru and stripped down and dove into the pool. I floated on my back looking at the stars, listening to the waves breaking on the other side of the dunes, smelling the moist Atlantic air and the honeysuckle damp on the night hedges. I left my clothes in the changing cabaña and returned to the house wrapped in a big terrycloth robe feeling like a king, feeling the way I most enjoyed, lucky and getting away with murder.

I wondered if that was what I as the girl in my dream had been doing—getting away with murder. If only I/she had been able to cut those wires around her ankles and run up Woodycrest Avenue filled with joy, instead of the deathly fear we had of being caught and punished.

# - 39 -

The following morning, we heard the nurse cry out. Instinctively, we both knew why. We got out of bed and made our way along the hall with reluctance. Caro was dead. She looked peaceful but I had to close her eyes. Her skin was still warm. Carmen began to cry. I asked the nurse and a maid who'd come in to leave us and inform the staff. I put the empty pill containers in the pocket of my robe and picked up the note left on her bedside table.

*Shaun,*

*Please forgive me. I did not want to go alone. That you and your wonderful girl are in bed together down the hall gives me the comfort I require. Call Dr. Cranley and Father Donleavy, both of whom have helped me with this and already forgiven me this final sin. Call my lawyer Jimmy Emory who has my will and burial instructions. I insist you have a bottle of Pol Roger in my honor this evening. Do not cry for me. Though I have done nothing of any importance or been of any real help to the world, I have had a long and wondrous life. Je ne regret rien!*

*Love,*

*C*

We sat there for a while. I slid open the door to her balcony, letting in scented morning air and ocean sounds that Caro could no longer smell or hear. I stepped out and observed another calm summer sea, then made the calls she asked of me.

We had breakfast in the kitchen where I made additional calls to some of my cousins on the compound to let them know. The doctor—who looked to be close to Caro's age—arrived, bringing along a gentleman from the local funeral home. The death certificate was filled in, signed, and witnessed just before Father Donleavy arrived driving a Mini. He was young and very kind. He blessed her and got on his knees next to her and silently prayed.

I wrote, filed, and paid for her obituary with the *New York Times*, the *Southampton Press*, and the *East Hampton Star*. She was buried two days later in the Southampton Cemetery next to her parents, not far from where my father and Scarlett's coffins rested under the sandy loam of eastern Long Island. During the ceremony I couldn't help noticing a Burger King, way too close by, just off the Montauk Highway.

The property and the house and all its contents were left to me along with what she had in the bank, plus an impressive stock portfolio. There was a request in the will that all the staff be paid as usual until their deaths, regardless of whether I kept them on or not. A second point stipulated that the house be maintained as it was, that it not change hands or be sold until my death, and that it not suffer any additions or architectural reformations—a clause, much to the surprise of the lawyer, that pleased me.

All this kept Carmen and me in Southampton for another week, and though some of that time was emotionally fraught, we managed to make the best of it. On our last night there before returning to Massachusetts I suggested we try some way of living together and she said yes. We celebrated by drinking more of the champagne

Caro prescribed, and we took a late-night swim in the pool after making love on the grass next to it. Corru barked and we ignored him. After Carmen fell asleep in bed, I lay there and thought about Caro and my father and Edwin Anderson. I made a mental note to try to find Caro's riding crop, but gave up the next day after a brief, half-hearted search. What I found instead were Edwin's letters.

# - Part Four -

*There seems to me too much misery in the world.*
—Charles Darwin

# - 40 -

Sept. 16th, 1967

Dear Caroline,

Our ship arrived safely at La Havre. From there we found another to take us to Gothenburg. Mother pretended to recognize it, if only for my benefit. It was from there that she sailed to America so long ago. We traveled by rail to Stockholm, and we are staying at a small hotel near the hospital. Mother continues to be in pain. Tomorrow the surgeons will remove the tumor.

We speak like Swedes from the past, I who have never been here, and mother who left when she was fourteen. People are amused by it. It will take some time to master the current expressions and more time still to become accustomed to living here. It does feel familiar in odd and unexpected ways. The food, the manners. It reminds me of when mother and I lived alone in New York, until I came to work for your family.

I will keep this small hotel room until she has recovered enough to travel. Then we shall go north to her family town. Although it has only been two weeks since I left Southampton, it feels like years ago. Perhaps that is normal for someone like me who has traveled so little.

*You made me promise to try to forget you, to try to find a new life for myself. I hope you will forgive me when I say that it is proving difficult. As a fifty-year-old man, born and raised in your country, a man whose only deep attachment, other than the one binding me to my mother, has been with you, I expect it will prove impossible. To be truthful, I prefer it that way.*

*Yours most sincerely,*
*Edwin*

*Sept. 27th, 1967*
*Dear Caroline,*

*I apologize for my silence. I received your letter ten days ago and treasure it. Mother's operation went as well as could be expected. Her recovery has been slow, and grueling, and she has only me to help her. She was in terrible pain after the surgery and even with the drugs her groans at night drew complaints from other guests. We have had to change hotels twice. Things are better now. We have come to her town, arriving yesterday. You can write to the address above, a cousin's house, until, thanks to the funds you provided, we find a place for ourselves.*

*I have held on to my sanity these past days thanks to your kind words, and thanks to my memories of us together. I miss your house, the land, and the beach. This town, Oppli, is as small as Water Mill, but isolated in the woods. It is already cold here at night. To keep myself occupied I assist a cousin of ours who is a carpenter. We mend chairs and tables. We plane floors and doors swollen from summer's moisture. How I've come down in the world. I suspect you will forget me far sooner than I shall you.*

*I miss the cars too. I miss the wines you'd bring. I miss your colorful clothes and the luxurious smell of you. I miss*

*watching everyone arrive for your parties from my window
above the garage, knowing you would come to me after Jimmy
got too drunk to notice. How you would sneak across the lawn
holding your shoes in one hand and a bottle in the other. How
your feet would be wet with dew and covered with blades of
cut grass. How your breath smelled of alcohol and cigarettes
and perfume mixed together. I remember it like a dream, here
in this place where liquor is so frowned upon and difficult to
purchase, where people eat bread with lard and smoked rein-
deer, where they wear the same drab sweaters every morning.
Yesterday I walked to a nearby lake, Lake Opplisjön, and
swam there pretending I was in Mecox Bay. The comparison
was so ridiculous it made me laugh aloud and swallow water.
What an absurd though fitting way it would have been to
drown.*

 *On the journey across the Atlantic I asked mother how she
met father. She told me she arrived at Ellis Island in 1900,
and though her brothers and her parents went west, to
Minnesota and Colorado, she found work quickly with your
family at their residence on Fifth Avenue. Like mother, like
son? They treated her well, paid her well, respected and edu-
cated her. They were unhappy when, two years later, she met
John August, the handsome metal worker who swept her off
her feet. After they married your father found my father a job
with the Consolidated Gas Company, working with chains
and cables for the tunnels being dug. It was hard work but
steady. Then they moved to Ogden Avenue in the Bronx and
mother worked as a maid for the Culhanes on Woodycrest.
Mrs. Culhane was also part Swedish and was glad to have her.
She stayed with them until she became pregnant with my late
sister Ingrid. Jimmy and his family lived on the floor below us.*

*He and Ingrid played together. Often, they played at being mother and father and I would have to be their baby. One day Ingrid pretended to breastfeed me, and mother caught her and was angry and made your future husband leave.*

*Mother said your family had been right, that she should never have married my father, that she would have become a proper woman if she had stayed with them, but that father had been so handsome and winning—at least at the beginning. And besides, she said, if she hadn't married him, she never would have had me.*

*What I never told you is that, after my sister died, father left us. I lived alone with mother for many years, until my early twenties, and by then I was a ruffian and a young man furious at the world. It was then she wrote to Jimmy and it was he and Judge Culhane who stepped in to help me, who got me to learn a trade and got me work with your family. This last part you know of course.*

*I must tell you. The guilt I felt betraying Jim's trust each time you and I were together was only bearable because of the pleasure of your company. I would do it again. I do not care if God forgives me, for I have not forgiven God for other things I cannot divulge even to you.*

*Most sincerely yours,*
*Edwin*

*November 23rd, 1967*
*Dear Caroline,*

*Here is our new address, at our own place, a one-story red house in the woods, within walking distance of town. It has been snowing for days and gets dark by 2 p.m. Neighbors call this time of the year the suicide season. It lasts until summer!*

*Mother knits and spends many hours in silence. I have*
*taken to reading, books from the local library, books in English*
*mostly. I recently finished* Robinson Crusoe *and identified*
*with both the shipwrecked Englishman and his man Friday. I*
*read* Treasure Island *and identified with young Jim Hawkins*
*even though I am now fifty-one years old—this a tribute to the*
*transporting magic of literature.*

*You are right, of course. I apologize for the blasphemy con-*
*tained within my last letter. I promise to keep my head and*
*heart high and exemplary, even during these months of cold*
*and darkness. And I will spare you the dismal facts about my*
*life that you ask for. They have no bearing on us, now less than*
*ever. I got into a fight at a tavern the other night with a*
*drunken man who insulted the United States of America. I*
*will not show my face in town for a week.*

*Remember the night we stole away in your Mercedes to the*
*parking lot by the Montauk lighthouse? Or have I dreamt it?*

*Yours,*
*Edwin*

*December 24th, 1967*
*Dear Caroline,*

*You are a naughty woman. But of course, I knew that. You*
*have even managed to get me in trouble from thousands of*
*miles away. The books you suggested I read have scandalized*
*the local librarian. I think if it had been one or the other, she*
*would not have been so distressed, but it was the tandem,* The
Confessions of Saint Augustine *with* Lady Chatterley's
Lover, *that produced a scowl on the woman's face I am still*
*fearful of. I found as I read the latter work that, true to a pat-*
*tern, I identified both with Oliver and Sir Clifford.*

189

*What books! Knowing the contempt in which I hold priests, you were brave to suggest Augustine of Hippo's text. And yet I found myself very moved by it. When I read these words, addressed to God, I only thought of you:*

*"You called and cried out loud and shattered my deafness. You were radiant and resplendent, you put to flight my blindness. You were fragrant, and I drew in my breath and now pant after you. I tasted you, and I feel but hunger and thirst for you. You touched me, and I am set on fire to attain the peace which is yours."*

*And then these words from the other book, the one the librarian handed me hidden inside a brown paper bag:*

*"Perhaps only people who are capable of real togetherness have that look of being alone in the universe."*

*And this:*

*"In the short summer night, she learned so much. She would have thought a woman would have died of shame . . . She felt, now, she had come to the real bedrock of her nature and was essentially shameless. She was her sensual self, naked and unashamed. She felt a triumph, almost a vainglory. So! That was how it was! That was life! That was how oneself really was! There was nothing left to disguise or be ashamed of. She shared her ultimate nakedness with a man, another being."*

*And this:*

*"All hopes of eternity and all gain from the past he would have given to have her there, to be wrapped warm with him in one blanket, and sleep, only sleep. It seemed the sleep with the woman in his arms was the only necessity."*

*This is what I dream of often, and when I awaken, when I look out the window and realize I'm staring at snow drifts obscuring trunks of pine, when I hear my mother wheezing in her sleep in the next room and remember where I am and where you are, my heart falls away from me.*

*Merry Christmas,*
*Edwin*

*February 11, 1968*
*Dear Caroline,*

   *Last week I borrowed Victor Hugo's* The Hunchback of
Notre Dame *from the library. I finished it in bed early this
morning. I savored it because it reminded me of the time
when, shortly after you and Jim put the television set in my
apartment over the garage, there was a show that came on each
evening called* Million Dollar Movie. *This program showed
the same film every night for a week. I remember seeing* King
Kong *and* Frankenstein *in this manner. Over and over again.
But my favorite film was* The Hunchback of Notre Dame
*with Charles Laughton and Maureen O'Hara. It coincided
with a trip you and Jim took to France. I was bereft without
you. I felt like Quasimodo. You were Esmeralda, the beautiful
wild gypsy dancer all the men were in love with. I was the one
who protected you and saved you, but then you went off in the
end with the man you truly loved, Pierre Gringoire, who in
my mind was Jimmy of course. I felt like Quasimodo for other
reasons too. My favorite scene—that I repeated in my head
long after the show had ended—is the final one when
Quasimodo looks down from his perch high above Paris. He
leans against one of the gargoyles. Peering down he sees that
you are happy and going off with Pierre Gringoire as the
crowd cheers. Then Quasimodo looks at the gargoyle and asks,
"Why was I not made of stone like thee?"*

   *The book is so different. In the book Pierre is a worthless
coward. In the book, Frollo, the horrible priest, hands
Esmeralda over to the authorities and she is hanged in a public
square. Quasimodo finds her corpse in a huge graveyard, in a
tomb on the outskirts of Paris where the condemned were
interred. He stays with her body until he himself dies. When*

*the tomb is opened long afterward and someone tries to sepa-*
*rate them, the two entwined skeletons crumble into dust.*

*The film is American. When I brought the book back to*
*the library and looked up the film, I learned the Hollywood*
*people built their own cathedral and medieval Paris on a*
*ranch somewhere in southern California. The film is sunny*
*and optimistic in the end. But also a lie. The book is real. The*
*book reflects life as I have seen it.*

*One of the reasons I love you so is that you are both—*
*American, sunny, optimistic, but European too, dark, passion-*
*ate, real.*

*Edwin*

*May 18th, 1968*
*The Grand Hotel*
*Stockholm*
*Caroline,*

*Only two hours have passed since we said goodbye. There is*
*a good chance your plane has yet to take off.*

*Rather than return north right away as I should—for*
*mother will be alarmed by my prolonged absence—she frets*
*whenever I am late for anything—I have come back here to*
*the hotel to write you from the lobby on stationery I took from*
*our room this morning. I want to savor a little bit more the*
*pleasure and decadence your visit has given me. Perhaps there*
*is a God after all, for clearly there are miracles, this one for*
*instance made possible by you, you who remain a true believer.*

*Were we really here? Might our suite upstairs facing the*
*harbor still be in the state we left it? The sheets a-tangle, the*
*bottle of champagne overturned in the watery bucket, the bath*
*still graced with remnants of your bubbles, the mirrored closet*

*doors by the bed reflecting our ravaged breakfast trays after*
*they reflected last night's frenzy of sin?*

*Now that I am alone again, sitting here in this plush arm-*
*chair, I feel out of place. I feel like an intruder who has gained*
*access to the lobby sneaking in through the kitchen, a wood-*
*man, a retired mechanic who will be asked to leave at any*
*moment. Your mechanic, your woodman, my Mellors to your*
*Lady Chatterley. But no, the common, vulgar cut of my jacket*
*does not betray me. One of the young men behind the reception*
*desk recognizes me, nods at me and smiles. The miracle*
*continues.*

*May your God bless you, and, as you Irish like to say, may*
*the Devil keep you. Though you would not let me say it this*
*time, it is very possible we shall never see each other again. But*
*then that is what we thought when I left Southampton. All I*
*can say for sure is that I am filled with renewed strength. I will*
*leave now, mail this, and stroll to the Central Station enliv-*
*ened and content.*

*Many kisses,*
*Edwin*

This last letter surprised me the most. How had Caro managed a
trip to Sweden? It was the same year I was living in Edwin's quarters.
The month of the Paris riots. I was watching programs on that same
TV set. I did recall that she and my father sometimes went to the
south of France in May. I supposed she found a way to break free for
a few days without raising suspicion.

## 41

Curious how these things can go. Carmen gave me the pleasure of her company on my annual summer visit with Caro. The two of them took to each other. This led, as Carmen put it, to Caro's "confession," which led, it seemed, to her elegant suicide. Her unexpected death put Edwin's letters into my hands. Her unexpected death delayed our travel plans.

We drove back to Lenox and returned to the Wheatleigh. Rather than just relax and have dinner at the hotel, which would have been the wisest and easiest thing to do, I insisted we drive into the village for dinner at the wine bar where I'd had that good Bandol rosé. There were only two little tables left, right next to each other. As we got settled at one, I was hoping no one else would come to take the other. But just when I thought we were free and clear, it was shown to a former colleague of mine from the Institute of Fine Arts in New York, a man with whom I'd never gotten along. This was a fellow who'd taken an instant dislike to me from the start. I hadn't seen him in years, and suddenly I had to make nice, introduce Carmen, and generally feel uncomfortable. Then I had to leave the table because of a phone call from my lawyer concerning the Ogden Avenue project, leaving Carmen alone with him. Had Caro still been alive or if I'd just decided to remain at the hotel where we would have had a perfectly lovely dinner, we never would have run into him.

"Can't believe he's finally got a serious girlfriend," he said to her. "How did you do it? He had quite a reputation. He was the most politically incorrect fellow in the building. He regularly warned students that he wouldn't put up with any gender, class, or identity whining, as he called it. The guy's got four billion dollars and was playing at being a professor. He took a dollar a year salary and made himself exempt from any committee work or department chairing, in return for fully funding half the new buildings at NYU back then, buildings he wouldn't let them put his name on. He thought putting your name on a building was vulgar and 'just not done,' thus seriously dissing most of NYU's other major donors and trustees. He had affairs and ruined a few marriages. And he hated putting up with other colleagues' children. Many times, at dinner parties, I heard him say that people talking about their kids was the most boring thing imaginable."

All this and more during the five minutes I was out on the street hearing about a local community group in the Bronx that was protesting the Ogden Avenue project's focus on an unknown Swedish immigrant from over a century ago. Reentering the restaurant, I could see Carmen had changed. She was still courteous and all smiles with our tablemate, but I knew her well enough by then to realize that something was up.

In the car and back in our room she told me all of this and I did my best to defend myself against the homewrecking charge. Yes, there'd been a time when such a thing had happened, but it was many years ago and ever since Scarlett got ill and we moved up here, I never went down that road again. Also, times had changed, and I was older. Carmen did her best to listen and contextualize, but I certainly understood her irritation and disappointment. I would have reacted just as badly or worse if I'd been blindsided like that. It put a huge damper on the night.

Before we each rolled toward opposite sides of the bed that suddenly seemed very large, the lights off, cricket noises coming through the screens, she said, "Look, I know you're older than me and all that. You've had your own life. We've both had unsatisfying marriages and more or less unsatisfying relationships. We met. We liked each other. It's grown into more than that, it's been a high, for both of us."

"It has," I said. "It is," I said. "I'm in love with you. I would never do anything to hurt you."

"You can't say that," she said in the dark. "We've barely started. There's still plenty of ways for you to hurt me, and for me to hurt you. And, you know, I know who I am, and I am devoted to what I do for a living. I'm a scientist. I'm very passionate about my work. When I met you, I was introduced to a museum curator and a professor of art history, a field I appreciate for all sorts of reasons and know too little about, a professor of art history who also happened to be very rich, and that was sort of fun and unexpected."

"But?"

"But I feel I've been swallowed up since then. I probably didn't need to know so much about your past so quickly. I've been immersed in it; the Bronx thing, your ex-wife, the houses you used to live in with her that, bizarrely, you've kept in pristine condition without getting rid of them or returning to them. I mean, there I was helping you get rid of your wife's clothing five years after she died. Even the trip to Southampton that was so magical in many regards was emotionally exhausting. It would have been better if I'd met you when you were into a real academic year, exercising your vocation, if in fact that's what it is."

"What do you mean?"

"Is it a vocation or just a hobby, something for you to do? I guess a problem for you is that you don't have to do anything. Is it true you have four billion dollars? *Forbes* had you at three. Whatever it is, it's kind of obscene. The life you led, that that nasty man described, was strange. And I didn't know you can't stand children."

I was starting to get angry and I knew that wasn't good. I knew this late-night, wine-mediated reckoning might end up being important, even fatal. I did all I could to listen, to keep my mouth shut, breathe, and then speak as calmly as I could.

"It's not a hobby. It is a vocation. That guy is just a nasty, envious asshole. I enjoy teaching. I enjoy organizing exhibitions. I can't help the fact you met me when I was on sabbatical, but I'm glad I was, because it brought about our meeting in Paris. I'm glad I was not in the midst of an academic semester, because I've had time to be with you. But I take my work seriously. I'm not the painter I wanted to be when I was young. I'm an appreciator, someone who feels that quality is important to pass along. I take my work as seriously as you do."

She didn't say anything. The silence was maddening. I went on.

"All right, perhaps the good timing that brought us together was also bad timing. I can see that now, and 'bizarrely' as you put it, it happened on the same day I had that dream, and all the dream has led to. I apologize for overwhelming you. I apologize for sitting on top of a fortune I haven't earned. I've been so excited since meeting you. I'm in love with you. I'd given up all hope of something like this happening to me, and if it goes south now because I've been crowding you too much, unloading too much of my personal crap on you, I sorely regret it. Isn't there some kind of reset button we can push?"

"How do you mean?"

"Like a take two."

"We'll see," she said. "Is it true you can't stand kids?"

"What I can't stand is the automatic worship of kids. What I can't stand is people assuming you are just as fascinated by their parenting as they are."

I wasn't sure where the kid thing was coming from. I went on. "I'm enthralled by you, in every way. I've never felt like this with anyone before. I know that's not cool to say, and I know you don't feel that way about me tonight, that's for sure, but . . . I don't know what else to say."

"You told me yourself you're always the one who leaves so as not to be abandoned again," she said.

"So, is this the battle royale you mentioned in Paris?"

"I don't know," she said. "I only know I don't feel good tonight. Something feels off. I feel like I've been railroaded into this, most of that being my own fault."

"I can't believe this," I said. "Everything has been great until now."

"We'll see," she said again, this time in a gentler tone. "I need to sleep."

And she did soon after that, which amazed me. I was too upset. I stayed awake for hours. I picked Corru up and placed him next to me. What was also irritating was that I knew she was right. I'd gotten her too involved with my past, and after the initial novelty of it, she was taking another look and seeing a guy possibly too far along in life, too stuck in his ways, and too eccentric. With a lot of money—there was that—but maybe that was not as appealing now as it had seemed either. She had tenure, a good salary, her own place, and her own life that'd been going along perfectly well until I came along. Then, just as I fell asleep, she woke me up. It must have been around three.

"We need to talk," she said.

It sounded ominous. It was the last thing I wanted. I leaned over and took a sip of water.

"All right."

"I need to tell you something," she said.

"Oh boy," I said in the dark, as if preparing for the worst. "Just—please—don't say anything drastic."

199

"It's something I should have told you before, something I need to tell you now for sure, for both our sakes."

My heart started to race. I really didn't want this.

"Go ahead," I said, like a man with his head on the block.

"You remember the guy in Madrid, the one who you saw when we were at Casa Dani at the market?"

I started to feel nauseated.

"How could I forget him?" I said.

"Like I've said from the start. It's not what you think. His name is George and he's my stepson."

"Your stepson."

"I told you my husband had two kids with a former wife, quite some time ago. The girl, who I never met, committed suicide when she was sixteen, and George is gay and about ten years younger than me."

This was a genuine surprise. It calmed me, just the smallest bit. For clearly there was more.

"Go on," I said.

"It took him a while to come out of the closet. His mother was very conservative, and Matthew is actually one of those antediluvian shrinks who consider homosexuality a disease. So, George got married, somewhat in the way your Scarlett was married to the guy before you. He and his wife had a child, a little girl named Emily. She was born in Africa, in the bush in the Congo where George was working. He's a physician, for Doctors Without Borders. Anyway, Emily's mother, who had no family to speak of, died giving birth to her. It was awful. And it was after his wife died that he came out to the rest of the world. It made Matthew furious, which helped fire me up for the divorce. And now George has met someone, someone he's serious about, a man I introduced him to in Madrid last year, and they want to get married."

I was feeling better and better.

"But?" I said.

"But Matthew, who disowned him, says that if George goes through with the marriage he'll sue for custody of the little girl."

"Is that even possible?"

"Probably not. But George has a new job that will keep him traveling a lot during what would be her school year and he just feels she deserves a more stable kind of childhood."

She was sitting up now, her back against the pillows and the headboard, her arms wrapped about her knees.

"He wants me to adopt her. He thinks a girl needs a mother and also, selfishly I think, he wants a fresh start with Paco, the Spanish fellow, who lives and works in London where George is going to live with him. We've been discussing it, seriously, for the past two months."

"Ah."

"What does that 'Ah' mean?" she said very quickly, defensively.

I remembered how she had wanted to have me adopt the dog.

"How old is she?" I asked.

"Eight."

"Does she know about this?"

"Yes. She says she loves the idea. I've known her since she was quite little. She can see her father when she wants, and she likes the idea of moving to the United States."

"And you?" I said.

"I've been all over the map with it, of course—which is why I've been reluctant to bring it up. I, like you, enjoy my life the way it is, and meeting you has added a whole new layer—of pleasure, I hope. But I love this little girl too, and I cannot leave her to be fought over between George and his father, and it may be the only opportunity I'll ever have to be something like a mother."

"So, you've already decided," I said.

"Yes," she said. "Which is why we're having this conversation. I can't and shouldn't keep it from you any longer. You need to know before we get into this any deeper."

"Right."

"I guess what we've been through of late, and then that creep tonight . . ."

"Right."

I really did not know what to say. I didn't know what I was feeling.

"I'm glad you've told me," I said. "It must have been hard for you to keep this bottled up these past few weeks."

I could see her nodding in affirmation. She was sniffling. I put my arm around her.

"And this is why you've been so sensitive about how I feel about children," I said.

"That's right," she said, very quietly.

She grabbed some tissue from a container next to her side of the bed and blew her nose. I raced through scenarios, with the kid, suddenly a trio, and without the kid, being back on my own again.

"I don't want you to say anything now," she said, "especially something supportive, because I may not believe you. I just wanted to tell you, everything."

"Okay," I said. "But it doesn't change my feelings for you."

"We really don't know that yet," she said.

When I woke later that morning, she was gone. There was a note on her pillow:

*Shaun,*

*I'm sorry but I'm still upset and don't have the energy to rehash things this morning. I need a break. And you need time to think about this. Knowing you have the other car here I'm driving your jeep to Cambridge. Hope you don't mind. I'll take good care of it. Let's take a few days off and see where we are.*

*xx C*

## 42

Exercising steely self-control, I refrained from calling or texting her throughout that first day, or most of it anyway. I stayed in bed for a while, stewing in my juices. I took Corru for a walk and had a late breakfast in the dining room. I called my real estate agent and told her to put the Williamstown house on the market too. If this relationship was to have a chance of working out, I owed it to Carmen to start from scratch, with a place of our own, chosen by the two of us, or built from scratch if need be. I owed it to myself. I wondered if they taught art history at MIT. I thought about maybe trying to transfer to Harvard or, going down a notch, to BU so that we could live in Cambridge or Back Bay and she would be close to her lab. Trying to get hired by Harvard, even with my money, would be difficult at best. Around dinnertime I initiated the following exchange:

*Did you get home all right?*

*Fine. The jeep is in a good garage.*

*Use it however you wish.*

*Got my own wheels.*

*I've decided to sell the Williamstown house too, as a gesture of mental health.*

*But you've loved that house.*

*Love you more. And it's the past. You're now. I need to be now too.*

*Makes sense, I guess. But don't do it on my account. Don't rush into something you may regret.*

*Miss you.*

*I'm off to dinner.*

And that was that. She didn't respond to any of my other texts that night and when I tried to call before going to sleep it went into voice mail.

She got back in touch the following day, by email:

*Shaun,*

*Am going to London tomorrow for a conference and to visit with Emily, George, and Paco. Then Spain to see my mother.*

*Xx C*

That was it. No emotional content. No suggestion of a possible when and where we might meet. No further comment about us. She was protecting herself and leaving the ball in my court. Or maybe she'd already determined I was a bad bet. I decided to use the time to go to Sweden. I wanted to see if I could find any further trace of Edwin. I wrote her back:

*Carmen,*

*Are you all right? You say nothing about us. Are we over? I sincerely hope not. It seems crazy.*

*Love and kisses,*
*Shaun*

I should have deleted the crazy line, but I didn't. She replied:

*Shaun,*

*Are we over? I hope not too. But please, let me breathe. I'm not crazy. We both need time to think about this and see how we really feel. It's a big commitment—for both of us—with risks—for the both of us, coming upon us too soon perhaps, but that's how it is.*

*Xx C*

It was something at least. But the old "I need some space" line didn't feel good, especially with it being asked for so early in the romance. My natural instinct was to be impulsive, to declare myself, one way or the other. But I had to recognize she was right. She and I both knew that some of my ardor, maybe more than some, derived from my believing, up until then, that her condition in life was similar to mine, someone childless and unencumbered. It would have been foolish and cruel, for fear of losing her, to say something too quickly. It might very well be something I *would* later regret. But how was one to know how we might fare together caring for and raising a child, one that neither of us had made, without at least giving it a try? In any event, I knew it was not the time to insist on any immediate solution. It was time to respect her wavering and her doubts.

*Carmen,*

*I will think about it with deep seriousness. Have a safe trip. You know how to reach me. I love you.*

*Shaun*

I drove the Citroën to the Clark and went to my office. I worked on my syllabi for the graduate students I would have in the fall, had a coffee with a colleague, and then drove for a final time to the Cole

Porter house. I walked the forty acres with Corru, went for a final swim in the pool—he didn't bark this time—and took a last walk through the house. The place was a jumble of old and new architectures that had been pushed together over the years, unified more than anything by the old slate tiles covering its numerous peaked roofs. It exuded a melancholy air. Despite our problems, my infidelities and her illness, Scarlett and I had many good times there. It had felt like a real home. Solid. Ours. Impregnable. Life was terrifying that way, attempts at permanence and longevity so regularly and piteously mocked. A few weeks earlier Carmen had been there with me, the two of us mad for each other without a care in the world, or so it had seemed, when the place had acquired a whole new glow that was now extinguished. I called Corru. We got back in the car and drove off.

I ordered a plane, packed at the Wheatleigh, and had dinner there. I used the hotel car service in the morning to get to the Pittsfield airport. I flew to Logan in a Cessna Citation and then in a Gulfstream to Stockholm. We landed around 8 a.m. the following day. I went straight to the Grand Hotel. It had, of course, been refurbished and redecorated since 1968 when Edwin and Caro had trysted there. I took a quick spin through the National Museum, had a nap, then a light lunch on the terrace of the Moderna Museet facing the Östermalm district. I ended the day walking around the old part of town with Corru and dined in my room. The next morning, I rented a car and drove north to Oppli, the little town that was the last place I knew where Edwin Anderson had lived.

I'd never been to Sweden and only knew it through Ingmar Bergman's films and Scandinavian crime series. My mother's grandmother emigrated from a seaside town south of Gothenburg, but that part of my ancestry was rarely mentioned as I grew up. What I saw those first few days was, alternately, better and more attractive, and then grimmer, than what I had imagined from afar. Many of the people were truly gorgeous, the immigrants as well as the locals. The architecture was functional, but cozy and inviting. The food was wonderful. I didn't understand a word of Swedish but virtually everyone spoke good English. As I got out of the city it got bleaker, with dreary roadside restaurants, ugly filling stations, and stingy-looking people in shapeless clothing.

Using GPS I found the one-story house where Edwin and his mother had lived, a run-down place in the woods painted the same Swedish red seen on so many houses and barns in the Berkshires. An elderly woman named Astrid was living there. She saved me a lot of time and trouble, what might have been a week of snooping around or maybe even hiring someone to do it for me. She told me that Elsa Anderson had died in 1970 and was buried in the local cemetery. The nurse who took care of Elsa during her final months was Astrid's sister Sophie, who began a relationship with Edwin. After his mother's death, Edwin returned with Sophie to Hudiksvall, where she lived and worked at a hospital. Edwin had given the house, bought with Caro's money, to Astrid. She told me that Edwin was kind and generous. She said her sister Sophie died of cancer some ten years later. Edwin continued to live in the apartment in Hudiksvall until he was unable, at which point he moved to an old age home where he died of emphysema in 1986. She gave me the name of the old age home. We had coffee and dark bread with a kind of crème fraiche on it. She was unused to visitors and did all she could to hold me there. Her clothing smelled of naphthalene, but the house smelled clean, like old pine, and the coffee was delicious.

I arrived in Hudiksvall in time to check into an unappealing Best Western hotel that had an over-chlorinated pool and an over-shellacked piney bar with bright lights and a sticky red carpet. I took Corru for a walk and we sat outside at a restaurant called Restaurang

49 where we shared a rather sad meal. I slept badly and went for an early morning swim before walking to the old age home that had been private when Edwin was there, and that was now part of the national healthcare service. I lied and said I was family and they showed me his record, a medical report, none of which I understood. But the nurse who gave it to me noticed an annotation at the bottom of the last page that mentioned a box of personal effects. She said that if I signed for it, they could give it to me and that they would be grateful, as they needed all the room they could get in their storage space. I signed the release, waited around, and then was handed what looked like a musty banker's box, tied shut with cord.

I thanked them, went back to the Best Western, and checked out. Then I drove south on a local road to the St. Maria's Chapel cemetery where Edwin was buried next to the nurse. Their graves were in a clearing surrounded by thick woods. The tombstone had his original name, Adranaxa Anderson. I stared at it as Corru looked up at me wondering what we were doing. What a long way Edwin had come—from Ogden Avenue, and from West 148th Street, and from Caro's garage apartment in Southampton. I took some pictures that I sent to Carmen, walked around a bit with Corru, then found my way to the E4 highway that took us back to Stockholm and the Grand Hotel. Rather than open the box right away, I took it with me to Paris.

# - 43 -

I didn't open it right away there either. I moped around for a few days bonding with Corru, who I took to the Luxembourg Gardens every afternoon, and once to the Bois de Boulogne. Summer was in full swing. I did my best to avoid running into Dirk or Consuelo and figured they were probably not in town anyway. Paris was full of Chinese tourists and pretty, half-naked youths sunning themselves on the Quays. I stared at them, entangled and devouring each other, as I crossed over the Seine feeling sorry for myself. Then, at dinner one night in the Marais, feeling bereft from hearing so little from Carmen, my phone buzzed. I retrieved it from my pocket and found the following message.

*I miss you.*

I felt like crying. I answered immediately.

*I miss you too.*

*Where are you?*

*Paris. How's it going?*

*Fine. Good. I miss you.*

*Can we see each other?*

*I could come tomorrow.*

*Can you bring Emily?*

*Really?*

*I should meet her, no?*

*All right.*

*I miss you terribly.*

*Sorry I've been so distant. I just needed this time alone.*

No one was sorrier than I. I wanted to cover her with kisses. I was also terrified of meeting the child but saw no advantage in putting things off.

*Send me your flight details and Thierry and Corru and I will be there to greet you both.*

*All right.*

Back at the apartment I opened a bottle of champagne and brought Edwin's box into the living room.

The cord tied around it looked to be a century old. The lid of the box had Edwin's proper name, birth, and death dates written on it in beautiful script. Inside there were just three items: a small, home-made doll, a copy of *Lady Chatterley's Lover* dedicated to Edwin from Caro, and the following undated letter, mostly typed, that had never been sent:

*Dear Caroline,*

*I hope you are well. So much time has passed. I can no longer remember how much you know and how much of this will be new to you. I believe I've told you the easy version of what follows, omitting certain unpleasant details. What I am about to put down here, what my mother told me on her deathbed, includes additional information that shocked me. I hesitate to write it and send it, for it is a sordid tale probably best kept buried with her. But since you have asked so insistently over the years, since we have loved each other so intensely, and since we shall never ever see each other again, here it is, in her own words, as best as I can recall.*

*"Your father and I were brother and sister. We were very close for as long as I can remember. When we came to America*

*with our parents, uncle, and aunt, we already knew we would stay in New York together once they moved to the West. We married to protect him, because your father was always attracted to other men. It was the way God made him. There was an incident in a bath house that was unpleasant, and it was only thanks to Mr. Cuddihy that your father was not arrested and sent to prison. That was when Mr. Cuddihy found me work with Judge Culhane and his family in the Bronx, where no one knew anything about us. Your father continued to work for Consolidated Gas, and I helped Mrs. Culhane with her children. She had memories of a Swedish grandmother and we got along. But the Judge took a fancy to me, and I was weak and loved him back. It drove poor Mrs. Culhane to drink. There were many ugly scenes. And then I got pregnant with your sister and stopped working for them. When Ingrid was born, I almost died of it. The doctors decided to remove my uterus. They did not consult me about it. They just went ahead and did it and told me I could no longer have any babies. I believed it was a just punishment for my sin. I remember telling the nurse that at least I had borne a girl, for that was what I'd always wished for. Your father, despite his proclivities, was a good father to Ingrid, and suddenly we looked like and were like a normal family. I stayed home and he went to work. He had his friends, and I continued to see the Judge now and then when the weakness overcame us. It was an arrangement that worked until your father decided he wanted a son. We fought over it. Even if I had wanted to I was no longer able to. When he threatened to steal one or to find another woman to try to have one with, I despaired.*

*"It was then that a neighbor of the Catholic faith who lived in our building consoled me and spoke to me about the*

*Foundlings of the Protectorate, babies born to wayward girls afflicted with sin as well. One day while your father was at work a priest came to visit. A police detective came with him. The priest asked me if I was a true Christian and I answered yes. Did I believe in Christ Our Lord the Savior and I answered, yes. Then he told me I might obtain a healthy baby boy—you my dear—not yet two years old.*

*"I was overjoyed. The priest stepped out and waited on the stoop. The detective remained and told me there were conditions, that when the boy reached the age of nine, he would have to return to the Protectorate for a year of what was called Special Education. I was confused, but in my excitement, I agreed and told the detective I would consult with your father. I watched the detective and the priest cross the Avenue and enter Mr. Valiunas's saloon. The detective was one of the men who later lied when testifying at Ingrid's trial.*

*"When your father came home, I told him what had happened and he too agreed and the following Saturday we took the trolleys north and walked the rest of the way to the Protectorate of the Archdiocese. The priest accompanied us to the foundling ward, and it was there I saw and held you for the first time. I never met the poor girl that carried and birthed you. You were a gift from heaven.*

*"The years went by. I taught you to speak and read in English. Your father taught you Swedish. Ingrid taught you games. The Judge brought both of you many gifts. Two months after your ninth birthday the detective returned and told us it was time to honor our end of the bargain, that it was time to bring you back to the Protectorate for a year. Your father asked him what Special Education meant and the detective told him it concerned spiritual matters, but that he should mind his*

213

own business. When we protested the detective showed us the document that we had signed seven years earlier. I promised to bring you the following day.

"Your father kissed you goodbye and went to work. Ingrid kissed you goodbye and gave you a small doll she made for you, one you often played with that was supposed to be you. I took you to the Protectorate. The manner in which the priest who received us looked at you gave me shivers. When he left the room to fetch another document to sign, I asked a nun passing by what Special Education consisted of. The nun bowed her head, made the sign of the cross, and scurried off. This frightened me so much I took you away again before the priest returned. I asked Judge Culhane for help but when he looked into it, he told me they knew about your father. I didn't know how. It was a time when people of his condition were sometimes tortured and executed in jail. I did not know what to do.

"On the very next day the detective came to our house to get you. I refused and screamed at him. When I did, he looked at Ingrid in the same way the priest at the Protectorate had looked at you. He told me that if I did not hand you over to him, I would regret it for the rest of my life. Then your father returned, and harsh words were exchanged, and the detective left. This took place on the fourth of June 1916. Two days later Ingrid was found in the basement.

"When the police arrived, they told us they knew who had done it. They told us it had been Mr. MacBride who lived with his sister in the building next door. We knew that MacBride, a simple man, was incapable of hurting anyone. We knew they were lying because MacBride was one of your father's special friends. Then the detective appeared and told us that if we did not do and say what the police wanted, the same

*thing would happen to you, and that they would arrest your
father as well for perversion and indecent behavior. Thus it
was that we lost our beloved daughter and were forced to
return you to the Protectorate. The Judge was inconsolable and
unable to express his grief to anyone but me. After that we
moved across the river to the other apartment you knew so
well. This was the year of the trial and the appeal, the sentence, and the execution of poor MacBride."*

Here Edwin changed to a fountain pen:

*So you see, Caroline, during my early childhood, I was
surrounded by sin. I did not know my parents were siblings. I
did not know Ingrid's father was Judge Culhane. I knew about
my father's nature, but it didn't seem to matter. When it came
time for me to go back to the Protectorate my father was insane
with rage. During my time with the priests there, the sins of
my birth mother were revisited upon me. It was only much
later that I learned that the girl who had carried me and
breathed life into me had herself been subject to the same treat-
ment. By the time I was returned to my parents I had ceased
speaking. For many nights father and mother fought and
incurred many protests from our neighbors. One night I told
her what had befallen me and asked her to pray for my sins. I
told her I was a sinner the priests were compelled to punish by
sinning against me, so that I might one day be forgiven by
Christ, Our Lord. When mother realized what this meant,
confirming her worst fear, she told father. He would not hear
of it. He cursed her and cursed me and cursed Almighty God.*

*He left soon afterward. He quit his job and built a shack
for himself in the woods at the northern tip of Manhattan*

215

*near the train tracks. He lived on squirrels and fish and pigeons. He drank and I would visit him sometimes and we would fish together. Mother was ashamed and did not go and see him ever, and when pressed, she told whoever asked that he had returned here to Sweden where he had died from drink.*

*I often try to imagine them the way they were when they left Sweden for the United States so long ago. He was a handsome young man, eager to make a life for himself in a Promised Land. Mother was fresh and beautiful, as beautiful as Ingrid would have been. They managed to find a way both of them could have a life in America. It was only his greed for a son that cast them from Eden. It was, mother said, as if the priest and the detective had been a two-headed snake, Satan himself, and that they had pointed out the apple to her from the Tree of Knowledge, the apple that was me, the apple she and father agreed to share and thus bring down upon them the Wrath of God. She said over and over how she and father had been like Adam and Eve, brother and sister, until the Devil appeared and drove them from Paradise.*

Here, he reverted again to a typewriter:

*"Dear Edwin," she said to me, "you have committed no sin. You have been sinned against atrociously. I was the sinner and I further compounded my guilt in the years you lived alone with me. After your return, after father left us, my Irishman, the Judge, then a widower but unwilling to marry me, continued to visit, he of the same race as those who wronged you, who lied to us, who sinned against children in the worst possible way, who violated and murdered Ingrid. But I could not help myself. He may have been Satan in yet*

*another form, but I did not care. Until we got older and he started seeing Mrs. Cuddihy after her husband died, he possessed me and filled me with pleasure of the most shameful kind. May God forgive me and may the flames of hell engulf me now as I deserve."*

Then, in pen and ink again, he continued:

*The irony of course is that I'm sure my birth mother was an Irish waif and my sire an Irish priest. I don't think mother ever considered this. And it was the Irish who brought me to you, dear Caroline. Mother and I were indeed possessed by the same race. Her affair and mine were the only true loves we ever knew. Had Mr. Cuddihy not suggested the position for mother with the Culhane family, Ingrid would not have been born, I would not have been chosen by them from the Protectorate, MacBride would not have been arrested, tried, and executed, and I would not have been saved later on from a life of crime and debauchery by the Judge and Jimmy who brought me to you. Is there not something poetic concealed inside such depths of misery?*

*Having told you all this, having come this far, I feel I must finish by telling you everything. Call it a confession if you will.*

Here, to my enormous frustration, it came to an end. He either never wrote any more, or additional pages had gone missing.

# - 44 -

I put the letter and the book back in the box. I looked at the doll—
the one, presumably, that Ingrid had made for Edwin—and then
I put it back in the box as well and put the box in the storage closet
under the stairs. I returned to the living room, sat down, finished
my glass of champagne, and poured myself another. My grandfather
the Judge, my mother's father, was Ingrid's father. Ingrid was my
aunt. I was Ingrid's nephew. The Judge had bedded down the maid,
knocked her up, and continued the affair for years. It was what drove
his wife, my mother's mother, to drink and death. For fear of scandal
they had been unable to save Ingrid, or MacBride. All the Judge had
been able to do was keep himself and his family out of the trial. But
neither had my father, his brothers, or his parents been called to
testify. Why? Edwin had been adopted. MacBride had been innocent. The police had been in on it. One of them had probably committed the rape and murder. The story was intensely more sinister
than it first appeared, and I was genetically connected to it.

I googled the Protectorate and was further stunned to discover
that the massive complex of buildings, where hundreds of children
had been kept and disciplined by Irish brothers and priests, had
been torn down and wiped off the face of the earth in 1938 to make
way for a planned community financed by the Metropolitan Life
insurance company. The community was called Parkchester. I
remembered the line in my Aunt Jane's letter: *By the way, you stayed*

*with Aunt Moira in Parkchester during the last week of your mother's illness and returned home after the funeral.*

Memories of Parkchester were chiseled into neurons folded above my optic nerves. The prison-like red brick buildings, the walkways between them, the artificial playgrounds, the lobbies and elevators, the parquet floors, the windows that opened using revolving levers. I remembered it as grim and depressing, bathed in Giorgio de Chirico light and surrounded by a neighborhood that felt like a wasteland. On the day my mother died, on the day she was buried, I was playing atop the ruins of what had been Adranaxa Anderson's nightmare, the Protectorate.

I wondered who the neighbor "of the Catholic faith" had been, the one who first told Elsa Anderson about the foundlings. I prayed it was not my paternal grandmother. But it might have been.

None of this really helped elucidate the dream. But it was all there, I supposed, condensed and entwined. I just wasn't smart enough to decipher it. And I wasn't sure what deciphering it would give me. Nevertheless, the dream had led me to revelations of things about my family that I hadn't known, or that I had deeply repressed. In the space of an hour I'd gone from being an interested but comfortably detached bystander, curious about some long-dead Swedish neighbors who lived in the building where my father grew up, to feeling implicated, attached to it by blood. Though irrational, I felt stained by it. Embarrassed. I was reluctant to tell any of this to Carmen, especially then, as she was preparing to introduce me to a little girl whose safety and well-being she contemplated sharing with me.

Their flight on the following day was delayed until early evening, but Thierry got the three of us to the Rotisserie d'Argent by 8:15. Then he dropped their luggage off at the apartment and went on his way. It happened to be Bastille Day and there was a lot of traffic. Eight-year-old Emily, who had never been to Paris before, was slim and dark and spoke with a proper little English accent. We shook hands at Orly. Her auburn hair was pulled back into a ponytail and her eyes were a very dark brown. There was a small scar on her chin. An impression I kept to myself was that she looked alarmingly similar to the girl in my dream. Settling into a banquette at the Rotisserie I told her how the restaurant had been so much cozier only a few years before when it had a different name and more seats and a fat house cat that sat wherever it wished.

She was talkative at first, as nervous as I was, and spoke a great deal about her father, as if to let me know she was clear on that, and then she asked me a lot of personal questions I did my best to answer. Halfway into the meal she began to wane and went into iPhone video game mode, which didn't bother me at all. She rallied with chocolate cake and ice cream. Carmen sat back and let it all happen. She didn't try to manage the encounter. When we left, Carmen held her hand and we crossed the Pont de Tournelle and went home.

Emily was agreeably nonplussed by the apartment. She immediately fell in love with Corru, who I took out for a walk while the ladies settled in. I gave Emily the nicer of the two guest rooms, the one that faced the river and had an eighteenth-century fireplace and a bed with a canopy over it. She and Carmen did their bathroom things together and we watched some of the fireworks from the living room with the window-doors opened wide. I kissed her goodnight on her forehead. Carmen put her to bed and read to her from a book she'd brought along called *Princess Cora and the Crocodile*. It was past midnight when Carmen came to bed. We made love, and it was intense, for many reasons.

I didn't say anything about what I'd found in Edwin's box until the following afternoon when, after an excursion to the Eiffel Tower, we returned to the apartment and Emily fell asleep. Rather than give Carmen a recap, I brought the box back out and handed her the pages. She read it through without any comment until she finished. Then she refolded the pages and handed them back to me.

"Wow," she said.

"Is that incredible, or what?" I said, nervous.

"She was your aunt."

"She was my aunt. The Judge, to me, was always an old man. I'd no idea about this side of him. They murdered his daughter."

"Raped and murdered his daughter," she said.

"And he and Ingrid's mother kept seeing each other," I said.

"Maybe they loved each other."

"The Andersons were siblings. The father was gay. MacBride was one of his boyfriends. It's all very twisted. I'm embarrassed by it."

"Why?" she said.

"I feel like a fraud. An imposter. I feel unworthy of you."

She smiled, leaned over, and kissed me.

"Don't be ridiculous," she said. "It's got nothing to do with you. It's fascinating and amazing, but it's no reflection on you at all. You know that."

"Even so," I said. "It gives me the creeps."

"This is sort of sweet, and terrifying," she said, taking the doll from the box.

We looked at it together, an old rag doll with little buttons for eyes. The eyebrows, nose and mouth, drawn on a face of canvas stuffed with cotton, had almost faded entirely.

# - 45 -

We went to Spain and spent a week in Madrid visiting with Carmen's mother. She was meeting both Emily and me for the first time. She was thin and elegant like her daughter. She had been liberal and progressive all her life, growing up in Barcelona within a conservative family. Her wardrobe was old school, sensible dresses and shoes and skirts that ended below the knee. The apartment, Carmen assured me, was classic haute bourgeois Madrid, sofas and armchairs upholstered in dark shades of green and burgundy, old family paintings, two walls of books, potted ferns, a tea service from France, and a collection of crystal water pitchers.

It was hard to discern which of us made her more nervous, the new American boyfriend whose Spanish was atrocious, or the young motherless girl who spoke no Spanish at all, and whose grandfather had made Carmen so unhappy. But we all got through it. On our last night I took everyone to dinner, returning to Horcher's. Emily behaved like a proper young lady and afterward allowed me to hold her hand walking back to the hotel.

Madrid was hot and dry. In the mornings we went for walks with Corru in Retiro Park before it got too bad. During the week the park was tranquil and spacious. The lawns were watered and green. Up until the middle of the nineteenth century it had belonged to the royal family. The Count Duke of Olivares had commissioned its construction in 1630 for Philip IV, employing Italian landscape artists. A great pond was built, the Estanque del Retiro, where Emily and I rented a little boat and rowed our way around. But by lunchtime it was a hundred degrees, and during the weekend the park was overrun with mostly immigrant families enjoying a well-earned day of rest. Carmen's mother—with whom we had lunch most days—was against air conditioning, so it was always an enormous relief to return to the Ritz for a major siesta in the afternoon. Sometimes Carmen would venture out at that hour, immune to the desert-like climate she'd grown up in, and walk around looking at the boutiques along the Calle Claudio Cuello. Emily and I would stay in the hotel room. She would draw or play video games and I would rest and read.

One day I took her across the street to the Prado and asked her to give me her impressions of *Las Meninas* and Bosch's *The Garden of Earthly Delights* and Patinir's *Landscape with Charon Crossing the Styx*. The only things that grabbed her attention in the Velasquez painting were the dog and the female with dwarfism. The Bosch painting fascinated her, but Patinir's was the one she most responded to. She said the landscape reminded her of England and that the man in the boat going down the river could be me on my way to see her and Carmen to have a picnic in a nearby glade. I found it curious and original and sweet that she made no mention of the rendering of hell depicted on the right side of the canvas. My students always gave it too much prominence.

We said goodbye to Carmen's mother and took a high-speed train to Barcelona and stayed there for a couple of nights. Catalonia certainly felt different. Reflecting its geographical position, it gave off a vibe that seemed a bit French, southern French. Though Barcelona appeared to be just as big as Madrid, its beaches and the steep hills behind it lent it a more romantic air. Many of the older buildings had facades of stone of a particular hue, a dark, ocher shade more elegant to my eye than the brighter brick and granite seen in Madrid. The culture and the people were different as well. The energized, in-your-face style, so prevalent in Madrid, was gone, and in its place there was an attitude more restrained. I suspected that both cities were more provincial than they believed themselves to be, but to some degree their respective appeal derived directly from that. I noticed in the restaurants we went to, a wonderful place called Igueldo, and another called il Giardinetto, that the service was calmer, and that what might appear to a Madrileño as standoffishness was simply good manners.

I rented a car and we continued north to the countryside of the Empordá where Consuelo and Lucia were summering. Consuelo's family had a big house there, what the Catalans call a *masia*. It was just outside a tiny medieval town called Madremanya. Dirk was in Ireland making his movie, an ironic, fractured-fairy-tale take on Jane Austen. Carmen and Emily and I stayed at a little hotel that was ideal: low-key and faux *rustique*, with good food and a lap pool, one side of which was lined with pomegranate shrubs. The girls got along, mostly, and every other day in the afternoons we drove to a cove, what the Catalans call a *cala*, for a swim in the Mediterranean.

One morning we went to the small city of Palafrugell, where Carmen and Consuelo wanted to stock up at a proper market. While they shopped, I sat with Corru and the girls under an umbrella at a busy outdoor café in the main plaza.

"Are you and Carmen going to get married?" Lucia asked.

Both girls were having fresh orange juice and chocolate croissants, a combination I found revolting, and they were teasing Corru by offering and then not giving him bits of the pastry.

"It's a bit early for that," I said. "We haven't discussed it. What do you think we should do?"

"I think the proper thing is to marry her," Lucia said.

"What do you think, Emily?"

"I don't know," she said.

I could see the idea made her uncomfortable.

"Well," I said, "we're not in any rush, at all. It hasn't even come up."

That seemed to put her at ease.

"I heard Mommy and Carmen talking about Emily's father getting married to another man," Lucia said.

"You did not," said Emily.

This sudden betrayal caught Emily off guard.

"I did too," Lucia said.

Emily started to get upset.

"Don't believe everything you hear," I said to Lucia.

"But men can't marry other men," Lucia said.

"Says who?" I asked. "Of course they can."

Lucia had always seemed so sweet and sophisticated for her age, and now she was behaving like a little brat.

"I've heard both my parents say it," she said.

"That's because they're old-fashioned," I said. "Men marry men and women marry women all the time these days. It's not a big deal."

"At my school it's a sin," Lucia said.

"Well, then you go to a really dumb-ass school," I said.

Emily pretended to be shocked. Lucia began to cry.

"Why are you crying?" I asked her, irritated.

"I'm going to tell my mother," she said in an unpleasant whine.

"Please do," I said. "And both of you, stop teasing Corru."

This got them both crying. I think it was all the sugar. An older couple at a neighboring table, French-looking, began to stare. To my great relief Carmen and Consuelo appeared at that moment, laden with bags of produce.

"What is going on here?" Carmen asked.

"Shaun says I go to a dumb-ass school," Lucia said, now really crying, milking it for all she could.

Both of the women looked at me.

"Now why would he say that?" Consuelo asked.

"And he said you and daddy are old-fashioned."

"I can explain," I said. "It seems your daughter has issues with same-sex marriage."

"She's eleven years old," Consuelo said.

"Well, that's kind of my point," I said. "She's way too young to be so uptight and judgmental."

The ride back to Madremanya was on the quiet side. The only benefit I derived from the unpleasant encounter and its immediate aftermath was that when we reached our hotel Emily asked me to go swimming with her. That was a first. By the time we drove over to Consuelo's for dinner, all was forgiven and forgotten. The girls renewed their friendship and Consuelo gave me a big kiss. Six other guests were there as well, including two men up from Barcelona who lived together and had a house nearby. They were charming and fun, and everyone had a good time.

Carmen and I made love in the shower that night after Emily fell asleep. In the middle of the night she came to our bed upset from a dream. Corru jumped up as well, making for a snug fit. When I woke the next morning only Corru remained. Carmen had taken Emily back to her own bed in the adjoining room, fallen asleep, and stayed there.

On our last night in Madremanya we took Corru for a walk after dinner through the narrow, agreeably ill-lit streets of the village. Emily and I played at imagining who lived in each of the houses while Carmen trailed behind, speaking with her mother on the phone. After Emily went to sleep, we discussed the rest of the summer and agreed to return to Massachusetts sooner rather than later. The academic year in the States started early and there was still a lot to try to organize. My real estate lady was putting together a list of possible places for us to look at and we'd need to arrange interviews for Emily at schools in Cambridge. A few days later we flew to London so that she could see her father for a couple of days, and then we flew to Boston.

# - 46 -

That fall semester was my last one at the Clark and at Williams. I closed on a house in Boston that needed some work, and a lot of commuting went on that autumn and winter between Lenox and Back Bay. But by St. Patrick's Day of the New Year we were living on Beacon Street between Fairfield and Gloucester streets, across the river from MIT. The only relic of note from my past was the Zurbarán painting rescued from 820 Fifth. The phantasmagorical image that had provoked such foul language from the whiskied tongue of Bunky Bass graced our entrance hall and was much admired. The portrait Carmen's father had done of her hung in our bedroom.

She was back at work, teaching and doing research. I had yet to find a suitable teaching position and was in no hurry to do so. I occupied myself giving three lectures at the Museum of Fine Arts, funding an experiment to provide courses in art history at the city's public high schools, and finalizing initial budget approvals for the Ingrid Anderson Foundation on Ogden Avenue. Channeling the Gino Colossi of my youth, I also took pleasure in dropping Emily off and picking her up each day at a school where she seemed to be flourishing. We celebrated Christmas in Spain, where Emily got to travel with her father and Paco to Granada and Córdoba, and we planned to divide the summer between Europe and Caro's house in Southampton. We were settling into a life that was new for all of us.

When I realized that spring break would take in the eighteenth of April, I—without much pushing—convinced the girls to come with me to Paris. My reasons were both sentimental and dark. It would mark a year since Carmen and I met, and a year since the dream.

Thierry met us early one morning at Charles De Gaulle and took us to the Quai de Bethune. The three of us had breakfast together and slept for a while and went for an afternoon walk with Corru to the Luxembourg Gardens. The chestnuts were in blossom. Holiday tables were under the trees. We had tea at the newly renovated Ritz, which I of course didn't like. The scruffy, stained-carpet version of yesteryear was much classier and soigné. I thought the facelift had turned the place into a vulgar watering hole for oligarchs and emirs.

On the evening of the eighteenth, Emily and Corru went to Dirk and Consuelo's for a sleepover with Lucia. We walked them over and had a drink. At twilight, an hour later, Carmen and I were back on the street alone. We looked at each other and smiled. We crossed the bridge and went to dinner at Itinéraires. We started with champagne and went on to a Chassagne-Montrachet with a risotto that had little bits of asparagus and truffles in it. We had a good time. Then we walked back home and made love in the living room, half on the couch, half on the floor, took a long bath together, and went to bed. She fell asleep.

Near midnight I got up and put a robe on and retrieved Edwin's box from the storage closet. I took it into the living room, opened it, and took out the doll. I reached in for the letter and read it again. Then I had a look at the copy of *Lady Chatterley's Lover*, a first edition published in 1959 by Grove Press that Caro had inscribed to Edwin. To my astonishment, as I thumbed through it and smelled the paper, the missing pages of the letter appeared. I was amazed I hadn't seen them nine months earlier. Three sheets of the same airmail-thin onionskin paper, folded razor flat and in precarious condition.

But as with the first sheets, the text was clear and legible. I took a deep breath and began to read Edwin's confession.

*On the third anniversary of Ingrid's murder, Father convened us and swore us to secrecy. Each of us lied to our parents that night about our whereabouts. There was me, there was Jimmy, because he'd been sweet on Ingrid, he was thirteen years old by then, and Gino Colossi. Gino wasn't actually chosen, but he found out somehow because he always stayed close to Jimmy even back then, and it was impossible to get rid of him. We were told to bring some kind of sharp weapon and wait at the bottom of Woodycrest Avenue. I remember walking down past the orphanage in the dark and being scared. Jim chose a knife from a drawer in his mother's kitchen. I took a screwdriver from a toolbox Father had left at home. Gino came with scissors from the family barbershop.*

*Father picked us up in a car. It was new and obviously stolen. We drove across the bridge to Washington Heights, then north toward Inwood. He was always direct with me about himself, about sex. He was Swedish that way I guess. During the drive he told us what he had found out. The other two boys had never heard anything like it.*

*"There weren't no bathhouses in Highbridge," he said. "We had no place to go that was safe. So we used the coal bin room in the basement of 1075 and 1077, me and MacBride, me and Albert Boulder, me and Paddy Culhane." Jimmy piped up and said, "Are you saying Paddy is queer?" "I'm saying he is a fine and gentle young man," Father said. "Ain't nothing queer about him. He just fancies his own kind is all." That seemed to shut Jimmy up, and besides, everybody had thought that about Paddy from the time he started getting whiskers. Father went*

on. *"Sometimes the four of us would meet there together. We used the quilt Albert kept in there to lie on. I was living with your mother then. Albert was married but hardly ever spoke to his wife. MacBride lived with his sister and brother-in-law, Conlan the plumber, who we all thought was one of us too, but too frightened to admit it. Paddy lived at home with his sisters and the Judge.*

*"The problem was Albert. Albert Boulder was Catholic. Paddy was Catholic too of course, but he knew how to keep things in balance. Albert was a holy roller and each time after we had sex down there, he'd go to confession and cry and beg for forgiveness. The priest he confessed to told the priest that worked in the Protectorate, told him everything, about me, about MacBride, and about Paddy. The Protectorate priest told Captain Morrison. They had the goods on us,"* my father said. *"They knew it all he said and threatened me when they came to take you back to that filthy place. You ain't that way, Edwin. I can tell. They were animals, these people. After they defiled and killed Ingrid and stuck MacBride with the rap, they threatened us too and threatened the Judge, to tell everyone what his son was like. MacBride was the sacrifice."*

*Jimmy and Gino just sat there and didn't say anything. "How do you know?" I asked him. "You'll see,"* he said.

*He left the car near Shorakkopoch Rock, the place where the Indians had sold Manhattan Island to the Dutch. We walked down through the woods, and then through an opening in a chain link fence that led to his shack. We were nervous but excited because it was an adventure. But we weren't prepared for what we found.*

*Two men were inside, their hands and feet bound with rope. Their faces were covered with blood and bruises. They were difficult to look at. They seemed to be dead. One was Captain Morrison, the detective who'd come to our house. The other was the priest from the Protectorate I'd come to know too well. "It was hard to lure them where I wanted them, one at a time," Father said, "but I did it. And now I'm done with them," he said, "or almost. Now it's your turn. For this," he said, kicking one of Captain Morrison's legs, "is the man who raped and murdered our Ingrid. And this sack of shit," he said, kicking the priest, "is the man who sinned against Edwin." When we were alone Father always called me Adranaxa. He called me Edwin that night so that Jimmy and Gino would know who he meant.*

*He made us drink some kind of cheap whiskey. It tasted awful and was hard to swallow but none of us refused. "Take your weapons," he said, "and stab them in the heart." He pointed to where their hearts were. Jim and I were scared. We hesitated. "Don't be afraid," Father said. "They's dead anyhow. I hit them with this until they confessed and then finished the job," he said, lifting up a length of bloody chain. "What they deserved for the crimes they did against Ingrid and you Edwin and poor Eugene MacBride and god knows how many others." Then, suddenly, Gino went at them. He leaned forward and stabbed both of them quickly and decisively, and not just once. He stabbed the priest first and then the detective. He stabbed the detective so hard the scissors came apart in two. Neither of the men responded, so we knew they were dead. Then Jimmy followed. I went last. Father patted us on the back.*

*We helped him drag the bodies out of the shack. He disappeared for a moment and came back with a conveyance he'd made from planks resting on a frame that moved thanks to a pair of bicycle wheels. We put the bodies on the planks and followed him as he wheeled them down to the water's edge. At one point the thing hit a rock and the priest fell off and we had to lift him back onto it. Touching dead men was harder than stabbing them.*

*The bridge connecting Manhattan with the Bronx, Inwood with Riverdale, loomed above. It was real dark by then. No moon or nothing. Father had us throw our weapons far into the water and wash our hands there. Floating in front of us, tied to a tree, was a skiff I'd never seen before. Inside it were all kinds of chains, some of them wrapped around large rocks. We helped him get the bodies into the skiff. The weight was such that the sides of the skiff barely cleared the water. He shook Gino's hand. He shook your Jimmy's hand and asked him to look out for me. Then he pulled me to him and put his strong arms around me and he kissed my head repeatedly. He asked me for forgiveness.*

*He untied the rope and shoved off. The currents between the Harlem and Hudson rivers are strong and dangerous. The Dutch called them the Spuyten Duyvil, the Devil's spit. We could barely see him as he rowed the skiff out toward the middle of the roiling water. We heard him doing something with the chains. Then we heard splashes. In too short a time there was nothing left to see but a vague outline of the empty skiff. Like Charon crossing the Styx, Father had chained himself to the vile bodies and taken them down to the underworld.*

*We walked all the way home in a daze and got to Ogden Avenue a little before dawn. We kept our secret ever since and never regretted it. Later in life Jimmy told me he decided to study the law because of it.*

*Love,*
*Edwin*

I got up and opened a set of the window-doors overlooking the river and pulled up an easy chair. I rested my feet on the sill. The Seine was dark. There were no lights on in the houseboats moored to the quay on the other side or in the buildings on the street above them. John August Anderson, the Swedish metalworker, brother and father, had possessed an Old Testament sense of justice, and the will to carry it out. He'd given the boys a curse and given them the gift of a dark secret. The experience pushed my father into becoming a lawyer, my father who'd been sweet on Ingrid and then ended up marrying her half-sister who gave birth to me. My father who became a prosecutor, thus qualifying to be considered a worthy enough husband for the heiress, Caroline Cuddihy-Woodward, which in turn facilitated my meeting Scarlett and inheriting her and Bunky's fortunes. The basic course of my life, the reason I'd been so fortunate, was put into motion by the rape and murder of Ingrid Anderson, the execution of Eugene MacBride, and the bloody killings of a nasty priest and a corrupt police officer by a chain-wielding Swede.

A nd as it had happened to Abraham, an angel appeared at that moment to remind me that I had seen the three friends together. Call it a recovered memory. It would have been some years before my father married Caro, and it took place, of course, at the Judge's house on Woodycrest Avenue. My Aunt Moira, the one with whom I stayed in Parkchester when my mother died, was married to a man who worked for 20th Century Fox. On that day, some cousin's birthday, he had brought a large projector and a print of their film *South Pacific*. We sat on cushions in the living room, the same room where the girl in my dream had cut the wire about her ankles.

We sat and watched the film ripple upon a white sheet affixed to the ceiling with black tape. Ever since my grandmother died of drink—because of the Judge's involvement with Elsa Anderson—and even though alcohol was his line of business, it was forbidden to imbibe in that house, and three of the adults had gone to the backyard for a beer. Edwin, handsome, tall, shy and solitary; Gino, short, dark, and quick to laugh; and my father the district attorney, the golden boy with deep blue eyes who'd survived the Allied landing in Normandy. There they were, reunited, drinking Budweisers while my cousins and I were entranced with the play of light in the living room.

There they were, chatting in the old neighborhood while my paternal grandparents still lived around the corner at 1075/77 Ogden Avenue. There I sat watching a group of muscle-bound gay men parading along a paradisiacal beach singing "There is Nothing Like a Dame." There I watched the musical unfurl, composed by two savvy New York Jews, inspired by James Michener, a progressive Quaker, surrounded by my mother's anti-Semitic, racist family. Much as my father had romanced Caro and I Carmen, there was the graying Rossano Brazzi seducing young Mitzi Gaynor.

There they were together that day in Highbridge, and I was with them. As palm trees swooned upon the swaying sheet, as the Pacific glittered before my eyes with Woodycrest Avenue stark outside behind it, I took into my being the image and voice of an aging swain, telling me what I now must do. *Once you have found her, never let her go . . .*

I put everything back in the box and stored it once again. I got myself a glass of wine, came back into the living room, and breathed in the river. I was in the Paris I loved, the banlieues hidden far behind me. I was in the Paris Fred Astaire sang about, "where all good Americans should come to die." An Irish kid from Highbridge lucky beyond his wildest dreams.

I took a deep breath. Carmen was asleep in my bed thirty feet from where I stood. Emily and Corru were asleep down the street. I realized I was happy. I knew it wouldn't last—but I was feeling it then, and I savored it. I knew that part of the earth would face the sun again in a few hours' time and kindle activity, needs, and conflicts. I knew Carmen would continue to fret about her mother. Emily would approach adolescence and give us worry. I knew enough about biology and physics to appreciate the mind-boggling absurdity of the universe. I knew the once-thriving bodies of my parents and grandparents, of Scarlett and Bunky and Caro, of the Andersons, of Ingrid, MacBride, and Edwin, of everyone connected to me who'd lived along Ogden and Woodycrest Avenues, were macerating in coffins. But there, in that moment, I was happy. I knew it

237

more than anything. If I had possessed some divine power to stop time, I would have done so then and there.

For the next few minutes it was still the eighteenth of April. I continued to stare at the river. I remembered how I watched my mother die when I was little, how I watched my wife die thirty years later. I thought of how I would be dead myself not too far in the future, and how, shortly after, it would be as if I'd never been. I knew how mean life was. I'd studied history. I'd read the books. I'd spied upon my father once making passionate love to a woman in our Bronx apartment. I'd seen him laugh, seen him kibitz with JFK on the beach, hit baseballs on the lawn in Southampton, swim in the sea. And then I watched him making a wallet, ineptly, after a stroke, sitting next to catatonic generals with unlit cigars in their mouths at Walter Reed Hospital. I had a rough idea of where this planet and its galaxy were in space. So, whether I had four billion or four dollars, I simply didn't give a damn about much else besides my own happiness and that of the loved ones I hold close to me.

Gerald Murphy got it right. Rich or poor, living well *is* the best revenge. My father's dirty secret was that he had stabbed Detective Morrison and the perverted priest before John August Anderson pulled them into the murky depths of the Spuyten Duyvil. My dirty secret was a devotion to the late paintings of Pierre Bonnard. For that was how I wanted the rest of my life to be, filled with tranquil and intimate scenes in beautiful homes looking out on gardens and the sea. Being able to contemplate Carmen in the bath. Waking up next to her at night with the windows open to summer thunder. Having toast with olive oil and honey in the morning with her. Watching Emily grow. Taking Corru for walks undisturbed.

And so as the clock approached midnight I thought, let's raise a glass to intelligent women and charming rogues, to children with manners, to people bored to tears by spiritual chicanery. Let's hear it for science and the arts, for humor and good food, for wine and sex. Let's celebrate empathic doctors and nurses and dedicated pilots, those who help the poor and underprivileged. Let's hear it for Mediterranean and Atlantic beaches. Let's hear it for dogs. Let's hear it for style and eloquence, for room service and dry martinis. Let's hear it for shadows, for Caro's riding crop and Belgian loafers. Let's hear it for the south fork of Eastern Long Island before all the arrivistes arrived, and for the five boroughs of New York City. Let's cut the wire that binds our ankles, and go back to Ogden Avenue when Ingrid and Adranaxa were alive, playing on the stoop with Jimmy and Gino, as the afternoon turned into evening, when it was almost time to climb the stairs for supper, before all the pain set in.

*PARIS, MADRID, WILLIAMSTOWN 2018–2021*

# Author's note

Much of the trial testimony appearing in this novel is taken verbatim from the 1912 New York State Court of Appeals trial: *The People v. Joseph J. McKenna*. The names and dates have been changed to protect the innocent and the guilty.